IMMERSIONS

ALSO BY KYLE MCCARTHY

Everyone Knows How Much I Love You

IMMERSIONS

A NOVEL

KYLE McCARTHY

Tin House
A zando IMPRINT
NEW YORK

Tin House

The characters and events in this book are fictitious. Any similarity to real persons, living or dead, is coincidental and not intended by the author.

Tin House is an imprint of Zando.
zandoprojects.com

First US Edition 2026
Cover and text design by Beth Steidle

Library of Congress Cataloging-in-Publication Data is available.

978-1-96310-870-5 (hardcover)
978-1-96310-878-1 (ebook)

10 9 8 7 6 5 4 3 2 1

Manufactured in the United States of America

LBK

For Assaf

Judith:
Ev'ry door must open, open!

—BÉLA BALÁZS,
Bluebeard's Castle

PART ONE

1

THE DAY I HEARD, IT RAINED HARD. LONG STREAKS outside my window, sleet as I walked to the train. Buses sent up sprays of dirty water, and the gutters ran fast and bright. Abandoned Christmas trees, lumped on the curb, grew sodden and dark. Deep in my boot, my sock slipped off my heel, but it didn't bother me: I was thinking about the news, thinking about whether it could be true.

The cold January rain followed me inside that day, making the lobby of West Twelfth slick, its carpets dank, the air clammy and close. So gray and cold and dark, the day I heard, that I was relieved to tuck myself away in a windowless lecture hall. Along the floor, everyone's umbrellas wept watery dark flowers.

That day, Chalmers's dress had two round water stains over her breasts, and a zip of darkened fabric down her front. As she lectured on *Jane Eyre*, she said the word *wife* a lot. She said *madwoman*, she said *money*, she said *slavery* and *beast*, but all I heard was *Johnny, Johnny, Johnny*. Outside, the rain picked up, pounding like someone wanting to be let in, and I shivered, glad for once to be with my fellow students, safe and dry and warm together. It was like a light inside me, this coziness, a light that pushed Johnny away.

Mira had been the one to tell me. She still followed the dance world; she would know. *Hey lady*, she had written. *Seems Johnny's back. Sounds like he's been back? Anyway. Hugs.*

Hugs. He's been back. Hugs. Johnny's back. Lady. Lady . . . All day I read it, all that rainy day. I read it in the halls and down the stairwell; I was reading it when I went around a corner and collided with two fashion design students, who giggled into their hands. I read it so long and hard it became a song my body was singing.

When I thought of him, I pictured him on the day you married him. A tall slash of a man, given to murmuring, with something frantic and fumbling about his hands. It hadn't rained that day; I hadn't even had the comfort of a bad omen on the day we gave my only sister away. Blazingly bright, the day of your wedding, and hot. Outside the church that morning the men's suits were a pale, uncertain black.

Funny things come back. I remember the rotten smell of ginkgo, and a fuzzy caterpillar squished beneath a child's shoe. I remember looking at Johnny, his dark swoop of hair and dirty fingernails, and thinking the thing I always thought: If he was so rich, why did he dress like such a dirtbag? Even on that day his suit didn't fit, and his shoes were the same work boots he always wore.

After The Brontë Sisters, I walked slowly down the stairs, the other students flowing around me.

Oh my God.

Mira fell into step beside me, shaking her head. When I didn't say anything, she added, You saw my text?

How did you hear?

Caroline saw him during intermission at the Hodge.

Another spin of the stairwell. Flyers for play auditions, for newspapers, for the Asian American film festival fluttered as we turned.

I hate him, I said.

We reached the bottom of the stairwell. A toothpick pretending to be a grad student slipped between us.

I've got to talk to him.

Mira blinked. Why?

He did something to her. I've always known he did something to her.

A line, crooked by half a millimeter, notched her brow. What does it matter now?

~

BEFORE YOU DISAPPEARED, you left many times. You came into this life practicing your exit. I came into this life losing you. Chasing you. Seven years between us: a biblical gap. I grew into your shadow; I grew to fit the shapes you left behind. I wore your clothes: a blue puffy jacket, a red velvet dress, a gray sweatshirt. I played with the plastic castle you had loved, with tower, drawbridge, and dungeon, a queen you could send tumbling down the chute. The queen is in the dungeon, you liked to sing, the king won't let her out.

A common game was dogs and owners: I was the dog, you were the owner, and my job was to follow you around on all fours, bleating out little ruff! ruffs! while you chastised me and fed me treats. In your old recital costume, the tutu around my knees, I tiptoed around the living room while the Moderato from *Swan Lake*'s second act blared. You taught me to play it on the piano: the first sixteen notes. I can still play it now.

You liked secrets. We had a secret language, and you convinced me that the trees conversed in code, that the squirrels were gossiping, that a goblin lived inside the radiator. Our toys spoke in tongues; you told me Blinky was giving me the silent treatment, and I believed you, I begged you to tell me what I had done to upset my doll.

Adults had secrets too. Between our parents hung electric wires. Furious whispers. A spatula thunked too hard, a clattering plate. Dynamite buried deep in the ground of family life. From above we listened, crowded together under my twin sheet, the hollow of your body making a cave in which I cowered.

What else can I say? You were bigmouthed and flat chested and when you looked at me I didn't want to be anywhere else. You bought me my first tampons and taught me to smoke a cigarette and helped me land a double pirouette. You were always leaving us, first slowly, and then all at once.

~

NOW ALL WE HAVE OF YOU is jam. Six blue jars lined up in our mother's pantry, with six blue silhouettes of sweet young nuns picking berries on their creamy white labels. *Confiture de baies. Abbaye de la Houssaye en Brie.* Each lid more dusty than the one before.

Every December a jar arrives, along with a card: Christ child on the front, your spidery script inside. *Sending joy this holiday season. Love, Sister Anne.* Your new name. On the envelope, our address in the same spidery script, a distant cousin to the cursive I tried so hard to copy as a child. PAR AVION stamped in red.

We don't talk about it anymore. Our mother treats it like another holiday card, leaving it scattered with the others on the kitchen counter. When we're together, we ignore it. But privately I can't keep my hands off it. Furtively I read and reread, looking for some message our parents missed. Nothing. *Sending joy!* After New Year's our mother dumps it, with all the glossy families and chirpy letters, in the trash.

I wish she would save the card. Or I wish we would eat the jam. But it is our mother's position that you are an adult and can do what you like with your life. Over and over she repeats this: Charley's an adult, she can do what she likes. Something savage in how she says it, something false. She can do what she likes!

Our father and I do not agree. We don't believe you were meant for the nunnery. Sometimes we blame the injury, and sometimes we blame dance, but mostly we blame Johnny. He did something to her, Dad will say, late at night, smoking his cigar in the dark. He did something.

What? What do you think he did?

Something. Something.

~

YOUR MARRIAGE HAD NOT BEEN GOOD. That was not controversial; even Mom conceded that. The marriage changed you, changed you fast. After that summer on Cup Island, you were different. More cautious. Subdued. You played with your nail beds. I had never seen you fidget before; as a dancer you had exquisite control. But now you picked at your nails, and when you spoke you trailed off, unsure of what you were saying. Whenever you called home, I'd hear Mom humming soft words of comfort. Later, at dinner, she'd exchange grim glances with Dad. But when I'd ask, How's Charley, what's going on, is she okay? I'd be told you were fine, that the early years of marriage could be tough, that they didn't want to tell me any more, they had to protect your confidences. I was too young to understand.

That fall, writing in the *Times*, a leading dance critic commented, *Charlotte Garbinski, usually so voluptuously wild in Luciano Fiore's boundary-pushing choreography, evinced a rare tentativeness. Her arms skimmed the periphery of her torso, as if protecting her chest, and her legs in the grand battements lacked conviction.*

You had never received a negative review before. Our parents and I did not discuss it. *Whatever*, you texted me, with a laugh-crying emoji. *Happens to everyone eventually.* But two weeks later, you woke unable to move your neck.

A herniated disk, concluded the team of doctors, cautioning that even after you healed, the snaps and jerks of Luciano's choreography would leave you vulnerable to paralysis. You took injury leave: four weeks, then six. At Christmas, you told us you were getting surgery. At Easter, you said you'd decided against it: Rest would be better. Johnny thought you'd better go to Europe. Some distraction, he said, while you healed.

For two years you traveled, and every time you called home, usually from a new city, usually to tell us you wouldn't be making it back for the next holiday either, our dad would hang up the phone afterward and say, Still running away. Not in his scornful voice, but sad.

It was good of Johnny to come tell us in person. I can still remember how he explained it. Carefully he told us first about your new love of cathedrals, how he had naively encouraged it, thinking it good for you to spend some time in self-reflection. That you called it *prayer* startled him, as did the Jesus talk, but once you explained that you never had religion growing up, that it answered some deep need in you, he understood. He supported it. But then it had moved toward obsession. Here we all tensed; everything moved toward obsession with you. In your boutique hotels you were rising at three in the morning with your rosary beads. Deep in the heart of Paris, you only wanted bread and water, a few steamed vegetables. You were reading Simone Weil. You were losing weight. After throwing out the clothes you had brought, you started wearing nothing but long dresses of black or brown. When he brought you to the countryside, hoping to distract you, you found a cloistered abbey and arranged a two-week stay. After emerging, you said you had heard the voice of God, telling you to consecrate your life to him. Soon your marriage had been annulled. Soon you had a new name.

It stunned me. It stunned me more, the kind of nun you became. Most nuns go out in the world, they perform acts of service, they teach, they minister to the poor and sick. They see their families. Not cloistered nuns. Cloistered nuns give themselves to a life of prayer, and I get it, Charley, I do: For a long time it was the closest a woman could get to being a monk, and who doesn't love that romance of solitude and simplicity?

But it's still the Catholic Church. That's what I can't accept. There's still all this nonsense about the temptation of the female body, and the need for nuns to shield themselves from prying eyes. Maybe you were tired of displaying your body onstage, maybe you were tired of dancing while others looked, but don't you see it's the same, only in reverse?

In that first year, when you were still permitted visitors and we flew to France to see you, I was frightened, Charley. The Lord in your convent frightened me, Jesus with his bloody palms and gaping mouth, eyes rolled back in terror. Ribs as bony as a dancer's. You stayed so calm in the storm of our father's threats and our mother's tears. In your eyes, visible beneath the white elastic of your novice wimple, I recognized the look of absolute submission. That airy fire, the steady blue flame. You had looked the same when you studied ballet.

For six years you have been gone; for five years you have been forbidden visitors. Sometime this spring, or summer or fall, you will decide whether to take the veil, and if you do, you will be allowed two afternoons of family visits a year. But when we fly to France and travel to that little stone room, we will not see your face anymore. Your hands will come floating up behind an iron grille, your voice will float out from the darkness of the enclosure.

Sometimes I lie in bed and try to think how many years our parents have left to live. I calculate how many hours, in total, you would have left with them, if you take this vow. I wonder, too, if I will keep visiting after they're gone, if my life will always be roped to the room and the grille.

I see it then: the cupboard of jam, slowly filling, one for each year. The sprightly nun with her berries, a flat cartoon, forever young, while behind stone walls you grow old. Will she do it? I ask our parents. Do you think she'll actually do it?

Time will tell, says the mother. Let her be, says the father. But what do you think happened? asks the daughter. Did he do something to her? Tell me what he did. If I knew, I could undo it. I could bring her back.

2

THE RAIN HAD STOPPED BY THE TIME I STARTED home, and the streetlight was streaky yellow in black puddles. I decided to loop north of Houston to give my blood time to settle. Mira had insisted on coffee and pastries at Vox's, and now I was all jangle and sugar rush.

It had helped, honestly, to have her there. To say a few words. *I'm kind of glad*. Those were some words. *I could punch him in the mouth.* Those were some words. The news didn't live inside me anymore; it was something shared between us. She told me what she had heard. I told her all day I'd been freaking out. Gingerly we held the news between us, regarding it.

Mira's good like that. The first time I saw her, she was standing at the barre in her worn leotard, squinting because she didn't have her glasses, mouthing the steps in the combination. She looked very serious, with her tiny face and short bangs, and a little silly. All semester I watched her, not because she was particularly good—she wasn't—and not because she was particularly beautiful, but because of a strange withdrawn quality in her face. Much later, when

I found out she had grown up in the city, this recession—a kind of privacy—made sense to me. A life lived among too many people had taught her how to close her face.

She was watching me too, that first semester. Everyone was, especially when the teacher asked me to demonstrate, as she often did. I shouldn't have been in that ballet class; I was too good. Girls from suburban schools took it, girls who should have quit years ago, girls who hoped ballet would help their tap.

I had thought that in a college ballet class I would be safely anonymous. I hadn't counted on my last name, said aloud during roll; I hadn't counted on someone like Mira, a lousy dancer but true fan, one of those obsessives who saw everything and knew all the companies. After the last class of the semester, she asked me if I was your sister, and somehow we found ourselves getting bubble tea. Though we were basically strangers, the intimacy of ballet, the hours of studying each other's body, made it feel like we had known each other forever.

You're a gorgeous dancer, she said. But why do you sometimes leave before jumps?

What? Oh. I messed up my knee.

So that's why you take class with us plebs.

Strange. She was actually starting to look different to me. That withdrawn quality seemed less like a retraction and more like a plug barely holding back an explosion of interest. Her self-possession was hard-won, and there was something wild threatening to overtake it.

You know, I saw your sister dance.

A tapioca ball flew up my straw.

I was really little, of course. My mom took me. She was like, the thing, right? She was the reason people went to Fiore Dance. And then when she—

Mira looked at my eyes, seeking permission, and I nodded. But all she said was, Well, it was so sad.

After that we were together all the time. To my surprise, she often smelled musty, like she hadn't taken a bath recently. Soon I understood that her smell was fitting. She was so busy reading, studying, going to shows that of course she would sometimes forget to bathe. I came to love her for her smell, as I came to love her for her loyalty. She was three years younger than me, and a year behind me in college. Love you like a sister, she sometimes said.

She'd said it on the sidewalk as we kissed goodbye. Text me, she'd said. Don't freak out.

Then I was alone again. Slowly I walked north, the news heavy inside me. He was here, walking the streets, his big hairy hands swinging. The gray, gum-splattered sidewalk crowded me, too close, and it was not the rush-hour commuters, not the kids juggling in Union Square, not the woman calling with leaflets in her hand, that made me hitch up my shoulders. It was him.

~

THE FRANKLINS WERE OUT when I got back. I dropped my bag, kicked off my shoes, and threw my coat on the couch. When our mother saw this place, she had sucked in her teeth and said I had to stop punishing myself. She said, too, that I should live with people I liked, not two randoms from Parsons who spent all their time cuddling in bed and liked me mostly because they couldn't afford a one-bedroom. But honestly I did not care. I let them sign the lease before I even saw the place. Took the smaller bedroom, too, facing the air shaft. I told Mom it was a place to sleep, nothing more, that I was out so much it didn't matter, and she was so relieved by my implication of a social life that she didn't ask any more.

In my little dark room I kept shedding. Pants, socks. Liberation from my damp long underwear that had clung to me all day, clung to me like the news, and even as I was squirming free I had my phone in my hand, tapping back to Mira's text. Then I was on my bed, fiddling on my phone, and then—before I had consciously decided to call home—I was listening to it ring.

Hey, sugar bear. How are you? How's it going?

In our father's voice, smoke and honey. A thousand crisp fall afternoons, a thousand burning leaves.

Good.

Words. They're weird, right? Dialing the phone, I had felt the news tender and burning on my lips, swollen like a bug bite; I had called (and I am never the one to call) to share the news, and listening to it ring I had thought, I'll say it right away, I can't wait to say it. As if by saying the news, I could hand Johnny off to him. But hearing my father's voice, I remembered everything. Our poor, tired, sad dad. In his voice was the house, dark and saggy with a creaky staircase and dust bunnies blowing gently in the steam heat; in his voice was his pipe, and the long nights, and all the time he'd spent longing for you.

How are classes?

I thought of Chalmers's water-stained breasts, the projected slides of sugar plantations. Fine, I said. They're fine, I guess.

Frances? He sounded alarmed. You're going, though, right? To class?

Yeah, yeah. I'm going.

Good, good. Because if you want to take a semester off—

I know.

But it's important that if you are enrolled, you go. It's too expensive not to—

I'm *going*. Jesus, Dad.

They must have fought recently about money. Dad didn't care about college; he certainly never cared that you didn't go. He cared about Experience, he wanted his daughters to be Artists, like him; never mind that he hadn't published any poetry in twenty years, that he spoke with bitterness of more successful colleagues, that he was still bouncing from job to job.

Honey? His voice was softer now. What's on your mind?

Nothing. Um. Yeah, it's strange. Johnny's back.

He's *back*?

Yeah, I think he moved back to New York. Maybe he's been here awhile.

Groaning steps and Dad's panting breath shush-shushed through the telephone as he walked up the corkscrew stairs.

You're still smoking.

I'm fine, I'm fine . . . His voice wandered. I could see him, looking around his study as if he'd never been there before. Like a dog, he had to turn around a few times before he settled. Now, what is this? You saw him?

No. A friend of Mira's saw him in the audience at the Hodge. They're saying he's moved back.

Wow. That's something.

But there wasn't the fresh outrage I had expected in his voice. He sounded tired.

I was thinking about getting in touch with him.

I'm not sure that's a good idea.

Why not?

A heavy sigh. Sweetie. Is there something you're hoping he'll say?

I took a deep breath. Maybe he's talked to her.

A suck of breath through teeth, the tinkle of ice. Frances. There are some things about the situation you don't know.

At the wedding something had happened that I still didn't understand, no matter how often I went back to that moment, standing outside the church in the hurtful May sun. That garbage smell of ginkgo, the geraniums dangling their little pink heads. The odd sharp scent of anticipation as we waited to process into the old Presbyterian church. Our cousin squishes the caterpillar, I think my thought about Johnny being a dirtbag. Everyone speaks softly, in muted tones. Crickets, somewhere.

The fight must have begun in those same soft murmurings, a mutter between Dad and Johnny, and in my memory it builds like the crickets' song, boring out of the background, until suddenly they are shouting and we all fall silent and Mom and Uncle Steve pull them apart. Fast, so fast. Our father's arms bend like wings until he snaps free and storms across the lawn. Johnny crumples onto his best man's shoulder. The ceremony is delayed half an hour.

Nobody explains it to me. After the reception Mom embraces Johnny but Dad walks away. The next week you left for Cup Island. It would be August before we saw you again, and by then you were different, you had changed.

Frances, Dad was saying now. You've got to understand, Johnny's the kind of man born with his boxing gloves up. He doesn't even know where he's swinging, he just swings. And you will remind him of everything he has lost. So please. Let it be.

I want to talk to him. I said it sullenly, like a child. Maybe he knows something. Maybe he could make her change her mind.

No. Frances. There's nothing he could say or do that

would bring her back. She's got to make that decision on her own. So please. Listen to me.

Tinkle tinkle went his ice.

Honey?

Yeah, fine.

Good. Now, sugar bear. Do you want to speak to your mother?

THAT NIGHT, as I was drifting into sleep, a horrible snap split the silence. A trap. There were a few metallic bangs as the mouse convulsed, and then silence. Through the wall one of the Franklins muttered, Oh shit.

In the kitchen, I saw the tail first. Long and curled, a fleshy white. The trap had done its work bloodlessly, and so the mouse's stillness in the harsh fluorescent light looked unnatural, its body slumped like a forgotten toy.

Shaking, I pulled on gloves, then nudged dead mouse and machine into a plastic bag. I walked the trash bag to the chute, then flicked off my flip-flops and went back to bed, trembling the whole time.

You wouldn't shake, would you? You'd say Gotcha, and relish dropping the body into the trash. I can hear the theatrical smack in your voice, the clang of lid against can; I can see your wild grin.

Or maybe not; maybe you're not like that anymore. You're a nun, you probably don't kill things. Maybe you'd be appalled at my setting mouse traps. Or quietly disappointed. Yes, that's how a nun would be. Forgiving, but detached. It doesn't sound like you, but I have to remind myself that I don't really know you anymore.

Anyway, if you're disappointed: I'm sorry. I didn't like it either. My roommates are slobs. I didn't know what else to do.

I often talk to you in my head. Can you feel it, across the ocean, the chatter of my internal monologue, explaining this and that, justifying, still hoping, after all these years, for your approval?

It's odd, I guess. We weren't close when you lived here. You were so much older, out of the house before I turned eight, always elusive, and then busy touring, and usually exhausted on your few visits home. No, we weren't close, but I always felt that you were my guide.

And now, with Johnny back, you had come closer, and I was chattering to you more. Deep under the blankets now, I imagined him writing you letters; I imagined your replies. Maybe he had news. Maybe he'd learned a clue, maybe he knew the secret words that would release you from your enchantment. The thought scuffled like a mouse in the wall.

3

MORNING. BEHIND MY HEAD, WATER WHISTLED IN the pipes. In the stairwell, boots clomped. The radiator made sounds like kernels popping in hot oil, then settled into a self-satisfied hissing. Rolling over, I touched sleep again, dream fragments drifting up. A train, forgotten tickets, and—the scenario came back with sickening familiarity—snow. Last night I was a snowflake, waltzing through a pine forest while the Tchaikovsky soared, and I did not know the steps, I had somehow forgotten to go to rehearsal.

All the time I dream like this. Back I go to the big black stage. Sometimes I'm a swan, sometimes a snowflake. The constant is the crush of girls in the wings, the swell of the orchestra, the panicked discovery that I never learned the steps. But the funny thing is that when I wake up, I'm glad I've had these dreams. They bring back a lost time. I'm dancing, and somewhere out there you're dancing too. You've never been in love, you don't know Johnny's name. At Christmastime we'll gather in the attic, with the barre our father bolted to the wall all those years ago, and we'll do our tendus together.

When I wake from these dreams, I ache. Once you know what it's like to move like that, you never forget. It's in your blood, and even if you stuff it down during your waking life it surges up at night. The body grasping blindly toward the pleasure it remembers.

For four years I danced after you disappeared. Of course I had to audition endlessly, but finally a small experimental troupe in LA—a vanity project for a French choreographer who'd fallen in love with a Hollywood starlet—took me on. The movie star would sometimes watch rehearsals from the doorway of our studio. Impossibly small, she held in the dark candle of her body such distilled charisma that she pulled us all toward her. Men and women alike would angle their dancing, ever so slightly, to the famous face.

It reminded me of you. You weren't famous, not like that, but you had the same concentrated charisma. You made people want to do things for you. In those years after you disappeared, when I was alone in LA, I danced like you were the one at the studio door watching. But there was a problem. I was angry, too. I was fighting with ballet, attacking it every morning in the studio, grabbing it by the throat and throttling it. Frances, my love, the director would call. Don't just do the steps, connect them. Make them speak to each other, my love. But I could only break them, and when I saw myself in the mirror, the rage on my face startled me. Soon the director started avoiding my eye. He knew I was the sister of the girl who had run away. Maybe he pitied me. Mostly I think he regretted hiring me.

When I went down in that fouetté I heard my knee before I felt it, a sound like cardboard getting crushed. Sometimes I still think about that last moment, my plié deepening, the music rushing. That tick of panic. Premonition like a smell. Then whipping into the fouetté. The crunch of knee. No pain, just falling. But even as my pointe shoe slid, even as I knew it was over, I flailed. I'm still flailing. I've never stopped. Slipping into the liquid dark of sleep, I sometimes jerk awake, as if afraid to let myself go. As if I am back in that fouetté again, trying to save myself.

I did try to come back after the surgery. But six months later I tore my meniscus, and after the surgeon had zoomed and clicked around the ghostly images of my torn-up insides, she said, Modern is fine, Pilates is fine, but you must never go on pointe again.

So two years ago I returned to the East Coast. At the geriatric age of twenty-two I enrolled in college. The other students seemed like children to me. College was unreal. I stood off to one side, watching myself buy books and take notes, flooded with the sense that my real life was happening elsewhere. It was like my ballet dreams: I had forgotten the essential thing in my life, I had missed something crucially important, and now it was too late.

Since Mira's text the previous day, this feeling had lifted. For the first time in a year I was standing inside my life again. As I stretched, cat-cowing and downward-dogging, waking up my body, the daily ritual, usually so mechanical, felt newly purposeful. Maybe by Christmas you would be with us again.

Memories of stretching together in the attic during holidays came back to me. Little groans as we swung into our splits, the click of your bad hip, a little suck of air in your throat. Lazy chat. Under the eaves everything felt child-sized, and the murmur of public radio from the floors below soothed us. I'd ask a question about épaulement; you'd tell me some story from tour, and I'd laugh and laugh.

Alone in my narrow room, I stretched my torso over my leg and imagined that when I straightened and opened my eyes you would be there, your legs tucked and twisted away, your collarbone jutting. The great drama of your body. You bemoaned it (You're a normal size, why am I so *epically* tall?), but I told you it was one of the best things about you. The critics said you ate up space.

After stretching, I opened my laptop. Johnny and I had never exchanged a single email or text, but the wedding had necessitated a blizzard of group emails, cheery missives from Mom, updates on hotel rooms and the rehearsal dinner, and so somewhere in my inbox—there it was. I copied and pasted his address into a new draft. Hesitated over the subject. *Hello*? No. *Hi there*?

Skipping the subject, I dove into composition. That proved more difficult. *Dear Johnny* was too formal, *Hi Johnny* too casual. We had not spoken since the annulment. *I heard you were back in town* was creepy; *an old friend saw you at the Hodge last night* sounded worse.

We had tolerated each other for your sake, we had been friendly, but when the annulment came through we were both eager to shrug off our relationship, like a sweater that never fit right. Now if I wrote to him it would seem false, and he would smell that falseness. Well, so what? I asked myself. So what if he didn't answer?

Johnny,

I hear you're back in town. Would you like to get a coffee sometime? It would be so nice to catch up.

Best,
Frances

Awful. But what could I do? My finger hesitated on the mouse. When I finally pressed *send*, I was thinking of the iron grille. I was thinking of your face, hidden in shadow. I was thinking again: He did something. He knows something. He must know.

4

I STILL REMEMBER THE DAY YOU CALLED HOME TO tell us about Johnny.

Your calls were an Event. I wish you could have seen the way Mom and Dad would drop whatever they were doing and dash to the phone. When I was little I had loved these calls, but as I got older I noticed how Mom sometimes literally ran to the phone, and Dad's fixed gaze as he rushed to the extension. When did they ever hurry to me? When was I ever an Event? I was boring, the youngest, left behind, always around. I didn't have your talent, I wasn't going anywhere.

To be honest, that's what I was thinking the day you called to tell us about Johnny. I came around the corner and found them huddled over the speakerphone. Heads bent forward, rapid nods. The glisten on Mom's lips.

Well, who would have guessed it? she said when they hung up. Sounds like your sister has met somebody. She met Dad's eye, and they both laughed, giddy as children. She's met somebody, she repeated. She's got a *boyfriend*.

Who? I said desperately. Even in that first moment, I felt afraid. Who is it?

He's taking her to Paris, Dad said, and Mom shook her head. Paris!

After that, we could never get a hold of you. The updates came late, breathless, scattered: You were moving in with him, you were off to Marrakech, to Tunis, then back to France. You were so tired on the phone that you were laughing, but it sounded like crying to me. I was fifteen, I didn't know a thing about it. You had met him at a party, you were in love, he was older and very rich. And then, on your finger, a ring.

When it's right, it's right. I remember you telling me that. We were sitting on the living room floor, surrounded by piles of bridesmaids' gifts and tissue paper and tape, and your eyes were glowing, your voice was loud, you seemed drugged or deranged as you insisted you didn't care about any of this wedding stuff, not the dress or the flowers or the cake, but Johnny insisted, Johnny had a traditional streak, it was really quite surprising, I'd see, I'd meet him soon. You talked so much about him, yet somehow you never said the thing I wanted to know.

Isn't it fast? I asked. Blood metal panic in my mouth. I mean, are you really sure? I kept asking. It seems like it's happening really fast. Are you sure?

You laughed, and said it again: When it's right, it's right. And Johnny— You seized my wrist. And Johnny, he makes the whole world light up.

~

PICTURE ME GLIDING UP AN ESCALATOR, ballerina tall, and striding into Penn Station with my ponytail swinging. Picture me at fifteen, consecrated to ballet like a monk to God. Still believing in justice, in the rightness and beauty of the world. Stepping off the train from Philadelphia, I was rehearsing the words I would say, sure I could save you, sure the wedding could be stopped.

At that steak house where I first met Johnny, you kept dropping your knife. It made me hate him. He mumbled, too, unable to open his mouth, and his eyes moved sideways. You were all nerves, not just dropping your knife but knocking over an empty goblet, and calling the waiter *sir*. Then you didn't finish your steak.

My first impression: Johnny seemed like a sad sack. An aging trust fund kid, pushing thirty and still a total dilettante. A do-gooder who made bad art. From Google I knew he occasionally showed what looked like shitty sculptures in small group shows. I also learned that his family had been in banking and real estate since their arrival from Holland three centuries ago, and that he gave a lot of his money away, mostly to experimental theater and dance troupes.

After that dinner, I drove our parents crazy with questions. Don't you think it's weird? I kept saying. We've only met him once. We don't really know anything about him. Don't you think a person should work? Why was he at that Fiore gala? What do we know about his past? So long and hard did I insinuate that finally Mom suggested I visit you in New York; if I got to know Johnny a bit I would relax, I would see there was no reason to worry.

God, I agonized over what to pack. Finally I took my sleeveless princess dress, even though the forecast called for rain, and my pointe shoes in case there was time for class. Before I left, Dad pulled me aside. Listen, he said. There's something I want you to do. When you get to New York—you don't have to make it obvious. But pay attention. Maybe poke around a bit. Ask her if she's happy.

Happy, I said cautiously.

You know, with him. He bopped my nose. Just see what she says. You two have always been close.

I might have been mad at you, I might have been despairing about the wedding, but when I saw you under the departures board, squirming and crooning my name, I couldn't keep the grin off my face.

Franny! You swooped me up in a big hug and rocked me from side to side. You're here. You're really here.

The whole subway ride you kept your hand in mine, drawing idly on my palm as you kept up a steady monologue: plans, last week's performance, wedding flowers. You were wearing jade earrings I'd never seen before and talking fast. Twice you asked about my train ride.

So, you finally said. Mom told me.

Told you what?

You don't like him.

She said that?

She didn't *say* it say it, but she said maybe you were having trouble adjusting to the idea of your big sister getting hitched.

Jesus. I buried my face in my hands. Mom.

No, totally, Charley agreed. She's a nut. And she thinks she's being subtle. That's the thing.

I do like him, Charley. I really do. Mom is insane.

Jesus, you're a terrible liar. You tapped my knee. This is our stop.

We emerged into a forest of glassy columns, strange boxy growth by the green river. This one, you said, and led me through a black-and-silver lobby lit by chrome wires. In the elevator, when you tapped the button labeled *PH*, my eyes widened.

Wait, so do you like live here all the time now?

I've still got the Eighty-Seventh Street place.

That was the apartment I knew, a prewar three-bedroom that you shared with a rotating cast of other dancers. Every time I visited, the house hummed pleasantly: Someone was always making toast, or sewing pointe shoes, or rocking on the foam rollers that littered the living room floor; someone was always in the next room, talking on the telephone. I loved the smell of that place, like body wash and banana and coffee, like dirty dance clothes and Tiger Balm. You complained about it; you hated living with other girls, always in your space, who fretted about noise and sleep. But I loved it there.

The elevator dinged and we stepped from its arctic light into the living room of a demented French aristocrat. There were stacks of books and orchids everywhere; the walls were covered with so many framed engravings I could barely see the wallpaper. There was a mauve love seat, a burgundy couch, a Louis XIV chair, and a poem written in pink across the bay window. Strangest of all, skulls—antelope, bear—with flowers where their brains should be.

We might go to his family's summer house, you were saying, but stopped when you saw my face. Yeah, you laughed. I know, it's a lot.

Before you could say more, Johnny entered with a private, funny smile on his face. Frances. You came.

Straightaway I was thunked against his great chest. A smell of soil, not unpleasant, but rich and loamy, rose around me.

Johnny, I said.

At the steak house he had treated me with an exaggerated winking formality, but now (without our folks around?) that formality mellowed into genuine courtesy. Let me show you to your room, he murmured, picking up my bag, and I followed him down a long hallway from which spilled many rooms, all a bit rococo (tapestries, embroidered cushions), but none as insane as the foyer.

The briefest glimpse of a snowy white bed.

Half a pace ahead he lumbered, shoulders rocking. Black hair showed above his ankles, black hair must grow on his chest. Dark, thick.

Johnny turned to me. I hope you'll be comfortable here.

A blue-and-white study with a sleigh daybed and a little en suite bath. My relief. Nights at home worrying about walking down some strange hall in my old T-shirt, knowing he was close, in the dark, that you were with him—no. I wanted to be far away.

It's wonderful, I told him, and our eyes met. An icy blue.

Back in the berserk foyer, I sipped Perrier and wondered what to say. You drew close to Johnny, and his long body bent toward yours the way his orchids bent toward the sun. You looked like doll bride and doll groom, shoulder to shoulder, perched atop a wedding cake. I remembered again the dark hair below the cuff of his pants, the snowy expanse of bed undulating beyond the ajar door.

He smiled. You okay?

~

AFTER SASHIMI fresh as a mountain stream, after eel and octopus and fatty tuna with bright white rice and pink pickled ginger, we walked to the Hodge. The Hodge! I didn't know then how well I would come to know it. When we entered, the ticket taker's eyes glittered with recognition, and the usher offered us programs with a private, satisfied nod. Walking down the long center aisle, I felt eyes on us, the subtle turning of heads.

At one point Johnny was talking earnestly to some old man, and we fell back. I sensed my chance. Hi, I whispered.

Hi, you whispered back, squeezing my hand. Having fun?

Yeah. Charley?

What?

Are you happy?

Yeah, this is great.

Two minutes into the performance, I became aware that my sweaty hand was stuck to the glossy playbill. As I broke free, the smack made you look over. Right. I was in your church. You two were solemn as supplicants; somehow, Johnny used his whole body to look at the dancers onstage. It almost made me like him.

At intermission we kept running into people you knew, women who wanted to touch you and tell you they had seen you dance, men who wanted to shake Johnny's hand. When you ordered two glasses of wine and the cashier caught sight of me, gawky in heels, she winked. Sisters?

Sisters, you confirmed.

Well then, she said, and drained the rest of the bottle into my cup.

~

AFTER THE SHOW we went to the Tulip, which sparkled with glittering towers of jewel-like bottles and flickering votives and a model-handsome bartender who greeted Johnny by name. Slurping a virgin mojito, I studied everything: the sliced lemons and limes, the smoked mirror, the waitress's geometric tattoo. You talked endlessly, eagerly, to Johnny about people I didn't know. You talked like you wanted to eat each other.

It was there, in that bar, that I got the feeling again. The black scruff on Johnny's neck looked dirty, then kind of hot, then nasty again. His hand was sliding up your leg, you were laughing and shrugging him off. You caught my eye and smiled gently as if to say Don't stare, and fury ripped through me. Something was not right. Something was rotten.

Later on the street you sneaked your arm around my waist, pulling me close. Sorry, you said with whiskey breath. It won't always be like this. It's love, love, love, you sang out. I startled at your voice, a silver spangle in the wet street. It's stupid loooove, you sang, and kissed my cheek, soft and sloppy, before running to meet Johnny at the curb.

~

IN THE MORNING you complained of feeling tired, and Johnny didn't bother to hide his satisfied smirk. It was Sunday, my last day, and you said we would go shvitz; from Johnny's wrinkled nose I gathered we would go alone.

Inside the banya it was loud and bright, people everywhere in robes or bathing suits sloshing past in big rubber shoes or slurping up tall cool drinks from the café. At the front desk, a man with a wild beard winked twice, once with each eye.

Show her the ropes. She's obviously a newbie. You, I've seen you here plenty of times.

The women's room was woefully inadequate, separated from the men's much larger space only by some scarred lockers and cheap wooden screens. Over this improvised wall I could hear men laughing, slamming lockers, snapping towels. I could smell them, chlorine and aftershave and fart. They felt so close. Knock too hard against a screen, and in they'd come, ruddy, pink and brown, glowing, hungry.

Silently we stripped. I sneaked glances. You looked stronger to me, muscles lining your back. Still long, though; still lean. Modern hadn't bulked you up. I was relieved, I didn't want you to change. Always, I had studied your body for clues; even before I understood what puberty was, I knew that your body was where my body was going.

Together we descended a narrow stair to a cramped, tiled space. On a bench sat half a dozen bare-bellied men beading sweat. The lighting: a cool, antiseptic green. Behind the bench lurked the plunge pool, deep and narrow as a grave.

I knew this was an important place to you, almost a holy place, part of the ritual of your week, like the Hodge. I knew that it was a compliment that you had included me, and usually I was happy to go anywhere you wanted to go; usually I wanted to be included. But these baths grossed me out. Subterranean, grimy, full of bare feet and sweat. And men. So many men. Their eyes flicked to you, pale and dark in your pink bikini, their gazes dripped like water all over you. Your thin, childlike limbs. The long muscles along your thighs, down your calf. The small high breasts, the shapely head, the long neck and big dark eyes. The features of a ballerina, the features of a child. My sister.

The room of radiant heat, you said, opening your eyes. Let's go there next.

I followed you to a wooden door. Beyond, a great stone room, with cement risers, as if for spectacle. Something cruel and ancient about it; something Roman. The heart of the baths, its pumping organ. The furnace glittered madly with coals. Unspeakably hot. We took our place among the other supplicants, sitting with our hands upturned on our knees, ready to sweat.

Soon beads of water were blooming on our thighs, soon the men around us were sighing. *Talk to her talk to her* drummed in my head. But I didn't know how.

I'm going to dump, you whispered.

As you approached the cistern, the lanky tattooed man beside me watched delicately from beneath lowered lids.

You stood filling the blue bucket with your back to us. So thin, so tall, like a reed. All my life I had been looking at you, comparing. Over your head you dumped black water, silver streaming down your back, and then you were shivering, a quick violent convulsion, the dark cap of hair smooth against your skull. The men feasted.

When you returned, dripping and panting, you said, God, that felt good.

Were you deliberately ignoring the sidelong stares or entirely oblivious to them? I dropped my eyes. When I looked up, you were eyeballing me.

Okay, talk to me.

About what?

You still don't like him.

We both have this gift, don't we? We read people. Their feelings come in, flooding. Basically, we're sensitive, and we were especially sensitive to each other. It was almost annoying. No hiding anything, ever. But I tried.

No, oh, Charley. No, I like him. He's great. Maybe I had some reservations after that dinner, but that dinner was weird, you know? But now, yeah, it's good. I'm really happy for you.

Bullshit, Frances.

No, I really like him. That sushi dinner was nice. He's a nice guy.

Come on, don't insult me like this. What do you really think?

I was crawly with heat. Teardrops of sweat dripped down my thighs. In a small voice I said, He's a little old.

He's a little old, sure. But eight years is hardly—

It would be like me marrying one of your friends.

It's really not that big a deal. That can't be what's bothering you.

Wasn't it? I began to doubt myself, there in the room of radiant heat. Wasn't it his age? Or was it this thing I could barely name to myself, the thing I only dimly knew? Was it sex? Maybe. For didn't I hate the way you touched each other, and looked at each other, the smirks over breakfast, his dark chest hair?

You don't like his money.

What? No.

No, you don't like his money.

His money's great. His money's awesome.

You sighed in frustration. Fine, don't talk to me.

My skin was tight. Water welled up from my calves, my elbow, the top of my feet.

Jesus, I'm hot.

Go dump. It'll make you feel better.

No, I'm fine.

I was baking, I would burst like a squash in the oven. Please, I said in a low voice. Don't marry him. You can't.

You looked at me more closely. Do you want to leave? Why don't you go dump some water over your head? You'll feel better.

No, I'm okay.

Just do it. You'll feel better.

Obediently I rose and went to the well. I could feel the men. Their quiet attention. The quickening. Then the weight of the bucket; the gush of water. Cold, cold, the breath whacked out of me cold, and I couldn't help but convulse as you had, wriggling while all the men watched.

You were tall, and thin as a reed; you were pale and dark, a racehorse, a ballerina, a whip. But so was I.

All this time, the men had been looking at me, too.

AT HOME, after a train ride where I sat, damp and hot and sullied, flushed, with rosy skin, I found Dad in the garden, pottering among the seedlings. Does it hurt them? I asked, watching him grip an uprooted plant by the neck.

Naw. You can be rough with these guys. He shook some dirt from white roots. So. How was your visit?

It was good, I guess. They seem happy.

They do?

Yeah. I felt myself on the verge of tears. And Johnny pays for everything.

That's good, he said, working the trowel. Nothing wrong with a bit of money. So you like him?

Yeah. His house is a little weird, but—he's nice.

I looked at him with drowning eyes, but I had nothing, nothing but a feeling.

~

FOR WEEKS I FORGOT about my bathing suit, wrapped in a plastic bag at the bottom of my book bag. When I finally pulled it out, late on a Sunday night, I found little spots of black mold lining the straps, the cups, the crotch.

5

ARE YOU OKAY? MIRA ASKED ONE MORNING. YOU seem amped up. She pointed at my bouncing leg. You're crawling out of your skin.

I'm fine. Carefully I slowed my leg and steadied my breath. I had an espresso before class. But really, I'm fine.

She cocked her head. It's Johnny, isn't it?

I don't care about him.

You've been like this since you heard. Frances, it's okay. He's not going to bother you. He's going to leave you alone.

My knee kicked up, and I settled it. Want to go to a show tonight?

What? Sure. Tonight tonight?

Tonight tonight.

I was going to maybe see Ben?

Ben was the older, meditative, deep and deeply troubled Zen Buddhist lately toying with my best friend's heart. Many nights we had stayed up late discussing him. Do you actually have plans? I asked. Like, actual real plans?

Of course she didn't. He lived to string her along as he

plumbed the complicated depths of his intricate soul. Come on, I said. Go with me. Give him a chance to miss you.

~

FROM THE BALCONY I drank up the audience, looking for a scowling dark comma of a man, tall and scruffy. But he was nowhere, or he was camouflaged well.

I sank back. Why had I ever thought this place glamorous? There were dead bulbs in the chandeliers, grimy baseboards, a tuft of cotton coming from the cushion of my seat. The peeling paint and water stains were not shabby chic, but blared a blunt truth: The Hodge was broke. They needed some of that Johnny money. They needed one of those famous big checks.

Why'd you do balcony? Mira asked. There's plenty of good seats down there. And then the narrowed eyes: Wait, do you think he's here? Did you get these seats so you can look for him?

The balcony is actually cheaper.

Frances. She sounded betrayed.

It doesn't matter anyway, I hissed as the lights dimmed. He's not here.

Darkness. Those last words hung in the air. Onstage, four women in gray smocks lay on their sides, heads cradled on outstretched arms. As one beast, they breathed, their ribs rising and falling.

When I had bought the tickets I hadn't paid attention to the troupe or bill, and I'd been so busy scanning the seats that I hadn't even opened my program, which meant that when it began I had no name, no handle, no context. Only four women.

In silence they rolled to their stomachs. Propped heads in hands. Collapsed. The music began, a pulsing beat.

Bit by bit they stood and slowly clambered into the world, like newly born things. Walking, they nodded resolutely to one another. One had the sense of a tribe. Once, twice, a dancer approached the footlights, standing apart from the others, and delicately pulled down her dress, revealing a bare shoulder. Then coyly she covered back up.

A new part: drums. From the wings they grabbed chairs and placed them on white *X*'s. Swiveling their heads, slumping forward and back, running their hands through their hair, the women convulsed, jerked by an alien force, *occupied* by a force as they repeated these most ordinary gestures. Sometimes flirty ingenues and sometimes mechanical robots, sometimes sexy and sometimes exhausted, they tumbled through the dance, sequences repeating, multiplying, dividing, and dropping away.

As I watched, I thought about being a woman, how it so often amounted to performing the rites of womanhood again and again, with joy and abandon, and then with weariness, with deadening. The women were doomed to finish the dance, as we were doomed to watch them. I don't know why the word *doom* seemed right, but it did. They were showing us—here is my neck, here is my hair, we are all alike, we must repeat this dance.

I knew it. I knew these steps. Why? It came back to me in a rush. A seminar room, a cold November day, the sky a steel blue, a dry chemical tang in the air. An old radiator, painted white, hissing and sighing and belching damp heat. I had been bored and restless, mentally absent as the professor blabbed, but once the video clip began, the Belgians, severe and beautiful in gray smocks, pierced me.

By now the women in the video must be close to fifty, with gray hair, grown children, regrets. In my mind, though, they were trapped in the video, forever tucking their hair behind an ear, pulling down a dress hem, shooting out a leg. Familiar young brides.

When the performance ended that night at the Hodge, I was lightly drenched in sweat. Wordlessly we filed out. No intermission, no chatter over wine. The severity of the performance seared me. I was ashamed I had come looking for anything else.

Mira and I parted with murmurs about how we couldn't speak, we were so blown away, we'd talk tomorrow, yes, kiss kiss. In a trance I drifted toward the subway in the stream of audience members flowing down the sidewalk, all dazed and bound together by what we had seen.

As I turned toward the uptown train, a set of footsteps drew close. I slowed, and from behind me strolled a tiny, precise man, the Hodge's program neatly tucked beneath one arm.

Even at first glance, I knew he had been a dancer. The economy of his limbs, the slight duck-like tilt of his feet, the eyes darkened with kohl. Maybe retired, but definitely once a dancer.

Incredible. Wasn't it?

He made it sound perfectly normal that we were speaking.

Yes. I blinked. Incredible.

Up close I could see he was old, with worn, creased skin, and pancake foundation clumped in the lines around his mouth.

I've seen a lot of dance, and that was something.

I shook my head. It blew me away.

Hesitantly, and then with eagerness, we chatted about the program, the dancers, the company. He knew quite a bit about the choreographer and filled in the hazy details I half remembered from my freshman-year seminar. I liked talking to him; it was easy.

You know so much, I finally said.

He smiled as if this pained him.

Do you go to the Hodge often?

Again that private, pained smile. Often enough.

His bushy brows were dusted with gray, like dirty snow, yet his lips were as plump and pink as a young girl's. Standing before me he flickered between old and young, male and female, with a face that might have been a carnival mask. Helper, trickster. I decided to risk it.

This is random, but you don't know a man named Johnny Fitcher, do you?

Johnny? Again that funny smile. Sure. Everyone knows Johnny.

Have you seen him? Despite myself I was talking fast. He was away for a long time, but now he's back, and I'm wondering—

Why do you want to find Johnny Fitcher, my dear?

That endearment like oil on my skin.

So you've seen him? You've talked to him?

He laughed. Johnny's not giving money away anymore, not the way he used to.

I don't want money, I'm not a choreographer or anything. I'm just wondering—have you seen him?

I have not. But I can tell you one thing.

He was a dancer, he had to have been a dancer, what with those limbs, and how he clung to youth, he maybe even had danced with my sister, knew her, listened to her confidences—I took a step closer.

I wouldn't bother.

I startled. Why not?

He's nothing like the man he once was. Losing his wife destroyed him. Made him mean. He raised his eyebrows at me. You do know about that, don't you?

I kicked a piece of trash. Maybe. I think so.

He squinted, and I prayed he would not say I looked like you. But when he continued speaking, it was in the same mild, almost bored tone.

But if you're really desperate, you could go to Aiko Ramen on Twenty-Third Street. He gets dinner there most nights.

He does?

The man looked at me sadly. Then with a little huff of air he turned his body around—it seemed to take some effort, like redirecting a ship, though he was not large—and began retracing his steps up the block. Good luck to you, child, he called over his shoulder. I hope you find what you're looking for.

6

I'LL SAY THIS FOR HIM: MIRA'S NEW GUY REALLY was a Buddhist. With his buzzed head and rimless glasses he even looked like a novice, solemnly nodding as Mira introduced us. Ah, he said, as if my arrival conformed precisely to some great unfolding plan. Ah, Frances.

Late February: bitterly cold, inky black. A night to spend at home with tea and novels, but when Mira texted to say that Ben was finally ready to meet me, I didn't refuse.

The ramen had not been my idea. It was Mira who had suggested noodles, who said it was so cold and dark that we all needed some miso or shoyu, and at that, I mumbled that I had heard Aiko up on Twenty-Third was really good.

What? Where?

This place Aiko. Someone told me it was really good.

Mira narrowed her eyes. Okay. If you want.

Five weeks, and Johnny still had not responded to my email. I told myself that that was that, there was nothing more I could do—for obviously I could not write to him again—but even as I was trying to convince myself to give it up, I kept thinking about the old man outside the theater. He couldn't be right; Johnny couldn't possibly eat at the same place every night. That was something old New Yorkers on the Upper West Side did. But then I remembered you telling me that Johnny did nothing halfway. He wrings everything out, you had said. He squeezes all the pleasure out of it.

Anyway, it didn't matter. He wasn't there. As Ben lectured and Mira gravely nodded, I kept scanning the tables and bar; I even excused myself to wash my hands so that I could take a closer look at a hulking guy at the bar who turned out to be closer to sixty than forty. But I was jumpy, I suspected everyone. I didn't know how Johnny had changed.

All through the meal, Mira barely looked at me: Everything she said, she said to Ben, her eyes slurping up his face, or darting wildly when he seemed displeased, which he often did (the scallion was not sliced thinly enough, the miso was not pungent enough, he suspected they had put pork in his vegetarian broth; this was not at *all* how it had been in Japan; did I know he had studied in Japan, long before we had even started college?). He kept trailing off mid-sentence, as if what he meant was too obvious to say, and into the silence Mira would be left eagerly bobbing her head. Then he ordered pickled carrots when she had said she wanted steamed buns. He made her suck his cloudy broth from his spoon.

Love repulsed me. Apparently he was always telling Mira he couldn't see her for a while, he needed more time to meditate, or chiding her for craving the illusion of stability when she asked what their "status" was. Whenever I suggested that all this Buddhist talk might be a way to avoid emotional involvement, she told me he was much too advanced to confuse detachment with avoidance. In fact, his dharma talks had directly addressed that fallacy. I had never heard her use the word *fallacy* before.

It depressed me. Together they were tacitly agreeing to misunderstand each other in exactly the right way so that this farce could continue. I sat with my face in a bowl of soup, watching Zen master Ben suck corn kernels while Mira stabbed and stirred as if certain that something real waited at the bottom of her bowl.

~

WHEN WE LEFT, the cold slapped our faces. Pedestrians walked the determined trudge of New Yorkers in bad weather: head down, shoulders hunched. I turtled too. At the corner I asked which way they were going, hoping to peel off and leave the lovebirds.

We'll walk with you, Mira said.

As we dodged a man dragging a sack of onions toward a cellar door, a couple caught my eye. Something about them strolling slowly through the cold with her head on his shoulder.

That whole mentality is about control, Zen Ben was saying. People want to believe that they're the author of their own lives, but the truth is that we're basically reactionary creatures. We just can't see it.

Yeah, no, totally. Mira squeezed his arm. We never know why we do what we do.

At the curb the man lowered his face to the woman's mouth, drinking her up. What was it? Not the face, large, leonine; not the hair, hidden under his hat. No, a style of movement, a hitch in the shoulders, gave him away.

Excuse me, I muttered.

As I jogged up, the woman and man turned in unison, a two-headed beast, the woman's face creasing with mild concern, Johnny's eyes widening in horror. Then his face became a pool of milk.

Later I would know well how emotion could splash over his face and instantly evaporate, but now it disconcerted me; even as I ran toward him, calling his name, I felt a chill at that milky blankness.

At the opposing green they strode into the crosswalk. Again I shouted his name. Strangers stopped to look. Somewhere behind me Mira was calling me, but when I turned to wave her off she had already given up and started falling back toward Ben.

By the time I crossed, Johnny and the woman were halfway down the block, not quite running but walking fast. It should have been easy to catch them—they were two, and I was nimble, unafraid to thread the space between parent and dawdling child, shameless about knocking the bags of an old lady—but Johnny moved like a fox, stealthy and low and quick, and his woman, graceful and nervous as a doe, picked her way through the openings Johnny forced in the crowd.

At Broadway I missed the light again and stood prickly and desperate as they leapt the far curb. Laughter behind me, dry and mirthless. A punk with a pit bull cawed, Let him go, let him go. He's got a new woman now.

Into traffic I waded. Cars screamed as if stung, but dance had taught me how to make myself tall, how to command a stage or street. With my hands out and my head high I halted a dump truck and a city bus, then reached the sidewalk and took off running again.

Johnny. I was out of breath when I reached them. Johnny.

What struck me: He was so *old*. (He was thirty-nine.) In the streetlight he looked worn and saggy, and at his temples there was gray.

Frances.

No displeasure in his voice, only the faintest hint of amusement.

I grew dancer tall again. I thought it was you.

Frances. Still with that faint amused smile. This is Gina.

Gina, a porcelain doll with fine dark hair, nodded but did not offer her hand, for which I was glad; I could not have shaken the hand of the woman who had replaced my sister.

Johnny. I can't believe you're back.

He'd gained some weight and grown out his beard, maybe to hide the faint lines that now etched his skin. He was bigger and shaggier, but he still had that same awkward posture, the same fleshy lips.

Yeah, I got tired of Cup. I've been back for a few months now.

How do you two know each other? Gina sized up my old coat, my wild hair. She looked like someone I used to know.

Frances is Charley's sister.

Ohhh. Reverence in her voice.

Sweetly I smiled up at him. We should get together. It's been forever, we should really catch up. Actually, I wrote you an email, I don't know if you saw it.

That would be great. I'm really busy these days, but—

But let's do it. It's been so long. There's so much to catch up on! I want to hear about your time away.

Subtly he angled his shoulders so that Gina stood outside the conversation. Let's do this later, he murmured.

Great, I chorused loudly. Great. When's good?

Email me, he said in a normal voice. We'll set it up.

How about this Wednesday? I practically shouted. Six o'clock, Café Lappet. You used to love that place.

I don't think I can—

You could make it. Gina slipped her arm through his. You should go.

I don't know if—

No, go. She's practically family. Gina grinned with all her teeth at me.

Perfect, I cried. So it's perfect. Six o'clock. Let's plan on it. Let's call it a date.

I'll look forward to it.

Before I could say anything more, Johnny turned away. With one paw he guided Gina back under his arm, and smoothly they glided down the sidewalk, her little head nestled again beneath his shoulder. White pebbles of hail bounced off my coat as I watched them go.

I knew then why she looked familiar. Her face was different, her body language too, but tucked beneath Johnny's arm, she looked how you used to look, held firmly in his grasp.

7

I STILL REMEMBER MY FIRST BALLET CLASS. I HAD to beg Mom and Dad to let me go. You, seven years ahead, blazingly talented, had beguiled the adults, so of course I wanted to go. But Mom's position was that dance was fine, dance was good, but dance broke too many girls' hearts; she didn't like the competition, the eating disorders, the stunted emotional growth, and anyway they couldn't afford two tuitions. No.

But when you began at the school downtown, it only made sense to enroll me. They couldn't afford a babysitter, didn't want me sitting around the school's lobby for ninety minutes. I was ecstatic. In the ballet studio at last, I found to my surprise that I was no longer a well-mannered girl. No, I was a fury unleashed, an animal loosed; I wanted size, I wanted speed, I wanted jungle cats and lightning storms. Snowflakes and flowers did not interest me, or any of us in that beginning ballet class. We were terrors. We were tiny blond and dark beasts; we were skinny knob-kneed girls, and when we took the floor, the floorboards trembled, the ceiling shook, and Miss Paulina clasped her hands and shouted over the piano, Girls, girls! You sound like baby elephants, girls!

Who cared? Tradition meant nothing to us. We didn't have time for Miss Paulina's talk about etiquette; we were circulating through the studio like a virus, we were back along the piano, down the canyon of barre and wall, gesticulating with upturned hands and splayed fingers, giggling when the piano crescendoed, and then running to get back to the beginning of the line, ready to once again make that diagonal scream.

Those were the best years. Before dance got hard, before I fell behind, back when I was pure possibility.

~

WHEN WE WERE DONE, wrung out and sweaty and slightly high, I'd pull on my sweats and sink into the doorway to the main studio to watch the older girls. Furious birds, your cheeks pink and your leotards sweat-dark, you did impossible beats and turns, propelled forward by the relentless piano, by Gloria's shouts, by some inner need to fly to the mirror. Oh, but I envied you all—you seemed both enslaved and free.

Even back then, at the more competitive school, I knew you would be the one to make it. At the top of your arabesque you lingered, hovering like a hummingbird, before dashing back down through the remaining steps, while the other girls jerked along, gamely trying to keep up.

~

AT FIFTEEN, when you abandoned Charlotte and baptized yourself Charley, I thought it suited you. There was something brash in your dancing, something daredevil and tomboyish: You fell out of your fouettés but you kept trying them. And you were so narrow, so slim; from the back you really did resemble a boy. Charley. Mom and Dad still called you Charlotte, and the teachers at school, but to the kids, to the boys—to me—you were Charley.

I liked your new name, but I did miss Charlotte sometimes. Charlotte had cuddled me and let me try on her pointe shoes; Charley was too busy, too impatient, stretching, sneaking a piqué turn in the kitchen, doing tendus off the back of a chair. Charlotte treated me like a pet; Charley treated me like a pest.

And Charley was wild. The day you cut holes in the feet of your tights, Mom cried. Fifty bucks a pair. You painted the holes with clear nail polish so they wouldn't run but they ran anyway, long stuttering ladders up your legs. You cut and pinned your leotards, you wore turquoise on a Tuesday when only black was allowed, you would not bobby-pin your bangs but instead sprayed them into submission, so much product I thought your hair might crack. You smoked. For a long time only I knew this. It became part of your smell, along with the hair spray and rosin and powder deodorant and sweat; it became part of your dance bag, the cellophane-wrapped box crinkling amid your gutted satin shoes. The day Mom found it—God, how you two fought. And the skipped classes, the tardiness, the missed pliés. It's for you, Mom shouted, and she was almost crying. It's all for you, this driving, these tights and pointe shoes we can't afford, Charlotte, it's all for you, and if you don't want it— A finger snap, a gesture that meant, Suit yourself, we'll get on fine. A lie. Something had changed. Now Mom talked too much to other mothers about her dancing daughter; she stayed up too late sewing pointe shoes, skipped dinner to drive car pool. She had fallen under the spell.

Soon I began to knot my leotard straps like yours and roll down the waist of my tights. I cut holes in the feet, too, and wore your old leg warmers, the ratty purple ones. Standing before the mirror, I sucked in my breath and pretended the two halves of my bony rib cage were breasts.

And then one Saturday it was done. An audition, three women and a man from Manhattan. Of all the girls in level D, you had been chosen for the summer intensive. In June, during an uneasy truce with Mom—her objections temporarily silenced by this success—you left for New York City.

You never really lived at home again. When you visited, an aura of strangeness, something at once big city and monastic, hung about you. Sharpened and purified, you were removed, your gaze going beyond me to some light I couldn't see. When Mom suggested you might enjoy taking a class with Gloria, you laughed. Do you remember? It startled me, your new hard plastic laugh. Then you softened and said no, you didn't think so. But you did go visit her, holding her veiny, age-spotted hands in your own, burbling your thanks, posing for a photograph, old ballet teacher and youthful rising star with their arms around each other, a crinkled snapshot that would hang on the bulletin board of the school for the next decade: Local girl makes good.

I could hear you at night, practicing your frappés, your feet gently whacking the floor. Every morning while the rest of us ate pancakes you stayed in the attic, clutching the barre that must have been too low for you now, diligently going through all the steps, creaking over our heads like an unhappy ghost.

When you were gone, Dad smoked his pipe on the porch he had built the year after I was born; Mom spent hours at the computer. When I think of them now, that is how I see them: Dad, sparking yellow in the dark; Mom washed in electronic blue.

They didn't fight when you weren't around. Weirdly, I missed it. When you were home, dancing and sneaking cigarettes and cutting up your brand-new tights, you were a problem for our parents to solve together, a situation to be tossed back and forth between them. Without you, they had no bridge to each other. They couldn't muster up the energy for their old screaming matches; instead, they were rarely in the same room together. They were deflated. They didn't know what to do with their hands.

And then: Lewis! Lewis! It's Charlotte! Mom would bellow, sending the dust motes spinning in the still, heavy air of our dark, narrow home. Lewis! Did you hear me?

He would get on the extension, and I would hover nearby, waiting my turn. From what I could tell, these conversations were never very satisfying. They were too short; they didn't have the right music. Mom and Dad talked too much; you must have been talking too little.

When I took the phone, it was always the same. You wanted to know about ballet class; I said it was fine. Your ballet was fine too. Can I talk to Mom again? Stunned, I would hand back the receiver. I was eight, nine, ten years old: Too young to understand that our relationship lived in our bodies, in our doing, in our games. We could hardly make small talk from a hundred miles away.

~

THE NIGHT WE WENT to see your debut with Fiore Dance, three industrial dehumidifiers were grinding away in the back of the house. The theater was small and dank, with squeaking seats and drippy black paint over the baseboards; even with the dehumidifiers, everything seemed slick. It made us tense.

Or maybe we would have been tense regardless. Six months before, when you left your apprenticeship at City Ballet to "explore" modern, Mom kept telling people it was a "phase." But now that you had signed your two-year contract with Fiore, Mom had stopped saying "phase" and "explore"; she would just laugh nervously. And this dank converted theater felt very far from Lincoln Center.

Looking at our parents that night, at our father's worn face, ridged like a walnut, and Mom's hands with their raised blue veins, and their bright spring clothing, Dad's lemon-yellow dress shirt and Mom's white angora sweater, I felt something like pity for them. I was twelve, and this emotion was an important discovery: Rather than fear or hate Mom and Dad, I could decide they were pathetic. Everyone around us wore black.

At some signal, three ushers shut off the industrial dehumidifiers, and the lights dimmed. In sudden silence, the show began.

In the first half, a troupe of barefoot women in white bodysuits gyrated blankly while a man in a suit wrote something in French along the back wall. And there you were, in the very back, frolicking inelegantly with the rest! Beside me, Mom breathed in shallow sips. We had been taught to carry ourselves like queens. Now you thrashed like a fish.

But what truly horrified our parents was the pas de deux, though they should have been ecstatic: For you to perform what was essentially the ballerina role amounted to an anointment by Luciano. But they didn't like your costume, that bikini-like thing, and they hated that your partner was older, gray in his hair, fur on his chest, with strangely plump lips that glistened under the lights. To staccato music you made love to the air beside his face. Spreading your bare legs wider and wider, like a snake unhooking its jaw.

As if gingerly but rapidly killing a bug: That was how they clapped at the end. Palm to palm, no fingers. Wincing. And when you finally came out afterward, that was how they hugged you, too: tentative and quick, as if the embrace might hurt.

You ushered us to some cheeky diner update blaring indie covers of last year's pop hits, and over a twenty-dollar plate of microgreens unleashed a steady monologue of Luciano this and Luciano that, Fiore this and Fiore that. Like children our parents listened.

It's all very sensual, you kept saying. Very sensation based, completely different from ballet. And yes, he really does cover up the mirrors! Even in rehearsal. No mirrors! He likes to say, I am your mirror.

As you talked, your hands grasped the air. It made you look haunted, unwell. Over their plates our parents exchanged worried glances. But there was pleasure, too, mixed with their concern. If you were in trouble, they could cluck-cluck over you again.

He likes us to really commit to the movement. Please, he likes to say. Please, I appreciate it when you hurt yourself.

And do you?

Do we what?

Your eyes darted to the door. All night you'd been like this, flighty, distracted, as if looking for a better table to join.

Do you hurt yourselves?

Oh no. Not really. Bruises, sure, but if you relax, if you trust and submit, really surrender to it, nothing hurts. You looked directly at Dad. You feel nothing at all.

~

IN THE CAR on the way back from the city, Dad spoke to the darkness in front of his face.

He seduced her.

Mom, driving, glanced over, pity on her face. In the dashboard's glow I could see her white throat. All its tendons. No, Lewis.

No, he seduced her. He's sleeping with our daughter. The way she talked about him?

In the back seat I pointed and flexed, pointed and flexed my toes.

~

OVER THE FOUR YEARS you danced for Luciano, we saw you do everything: perform in a nude bodysuit, smear mud on your face, run repeatedly into a brick wall. Luciano liked to take something ordinary—a kiss, a slap, a sneeze—and exaggerate it until the violence showed. He liked the inside of a thigh; he liked impossible contortions, exploding steps, the frank eyeball of the audience. If our parents still disapproved, they never said, though sometimes, when Dad was alone, I caught him staring into space, his lips moving rapidly, soundlessly, as if rehearsing an argument in his head.

Luciano, Luciano—and then, all at once, Johnny.

8

SO. TONIGHT, YEAH?

Tonight.

Mira grimaced. You're having dinner?

Drinks. At Café Lappet.

We headed toward the Fifth Avenue building, Mira chewing the inside of her cheek. At the crosswalk I studied her. Her nose belonged on a Roman coin, her forehead deserved a diadem. She had hazel in her eyes, copper in her skin; usually she glowed, but now, worry had dulled and creased her face.

You disapprove, I said.

I don't understand. That's different. I don't get it. This whole time I've been confused, honestly. You basically hate this guy, right? I mean, you've always said you blamed him for what happened. So why are you chasing after him? Why did you like literally run him down?

Charley's taking her vows this year. This is the year she decides. This is her last chance to change her mind.

Mira cocked an eyebrow. You think he knows something?

Maybe he's talked to her. Or maybe he'll tell me something about what happened between them. I don't know. He's my only link to my sister.

She stopped and tapped me on the breastbone. You're the link. She's your sister.

I shrugged off her fingers. It doesn't feel that way.

~

CAFÉ LAPPET WAS ALL WRONG. A world of white tablecloths and red leather booths, of bartenders in tuxedos and pyramids of lemons and limes. Couples breathing sex over big bloody steaks. The air soft with jazz and money. As I followed the host back and back, the restaurant endlessly doubled in mirrors, my eyes landed on a lone woman voluptuously smearing a snowy napkin across her face. Briefly, our eyes met as I walked past.

The host coughed. Here we are. I startled. A woman sat beside Johnny in the booth.

Franny, Johnny chimed, rising; he had never called me that before, and his kiss on my cheek felt showy and strange. This is my dear, dear old friend Tess.

Frances, the woman cooed, opening her arms. Are you a hugging person? I can't not hug. I'm a hugging person. C'mere.

In her arms I felt alarmed. It surprised me that she was around Johnny's age, though I thought she was pretty, small and dark with a heart-shaped face. It's so good to meet you, she hummed.

Once we were settled, Johnny ordered a martini and Tess said she would take a whiskey sour. I closed my eyes. When I opened them, everyone was looking at me. Asking for a drink—asking for the same drink as this strange woman—felt like defeat. Yet that is what I did.

Frances. Tess took my hand in hers. Her hands were cool and smooth, almost oily. I've heard so much about you. Her fingers wrapped around mine, aggressive, insistent.

Johnny's face was expressionless.

You're in school, aren't you? What are you studying?

English, I said cautiously. With a minor in dance. Dance history, not studio practice.

Mmmh, mmmh. Her face was an overripe peach, as if rather than aging she was going soft. But you dance, like your sister?

Not exactly like her.

Tess pouted.

The drinks arrived brimming. Johnny jerked up his martini glass, ignored the gin that splashed his knuckles, and proposed a toast: To us!

To us! I repeated weakly, and we jutted out our necks and sipped like birds.

When we lowered our glasses, Tess took Johnny's hand. Bandages circled his knuckles, gray and stained. How's it feeling?

You hurt your hand! I exclaimed, and they both looked over at me: Now I was the uncouth one.

Better. I can still do all the important stuff, he said, and—so quick I nearly missed it—stroked the air obscenely. Tess swatted him, laughing.

How did you hurt your hand?

Johnny took a big swallow. Somewhere a bartender was dully shaking a drink. I punched a wall. He showed his yellow canines. I've got a terrible temper.

He made it sound like a bad, if minor, habit. *I'm terrible about flossing my teeth.*

I sipped my whiskey sour. Too sweet. Tess and Johnny began talking about some art show they had both seen; urgently Johnny stabbed the air, making some point, and Tess argued right back. Their eyes gleamed, their lips grew wet.

How like Johnny, I thought. How perfectly like him. Back when you were with him, it bothered me how much he loved "intellectual discourse," how easily he launched into his new ideas. Apparently he hadn't changed. *I punched a wall.* Now, two minutes later, they were discussing something else.

Sorry, what are you talking about?

They looked over.

I didn't see it. The show. Or whatever. What was it?

Oh no. Tess collapsed into theatrical giggles, seizing Johnny's uninjured hand. Oh no. Johnny. We're being terrible. We're being the *worst.* You've got to excuse us. When we see each other, we get to jabbering, but enough, enough.

She let go of Johnny's hand to seize mine; she really was a toucher, a grabber. Frances. Tell me about yourself.

She began to pepper me with questions again, about college and the Franklins and what, exactly, I thought about Marina Abramović, playing the part of my eccentric aunt. Meanwhile Johnny listened solemnly. They were ganging up on me; I felt it distinctly. He had brought her along to stop me from asking questions. Every time I turned to Johnny, Tess asked me something else.

Finally she took a gulp of her drink, and I slipped Johnny a question about Cup Island.

His face darkened. I was basically hiding out. I think I was really depressed.

You were there a long time.

Johnny coughed, looking down at the tablecloth. Six years. But I was back and forth a lot. Connecticut's not far.

Hurriedly I said, It's good you came back. You can't run away forever.

Very wise. Tess bobbed her head. Very wise. You're so mature, Frances! How'd you get to be so grown up?

A silence in which we all again heard the sound of your name.

Excuse me, Johnny muttered, lumbering off to the restrooms.

In the silence after his departure, I became aware that Café Lappet was filling up. The air was hectic, everyone drinking in a blurred, frantic way. Tess turned to me. It's such a shame, what happened, she said, her voice low and confidential. Not that I didn't see it coming.

For a split second I thought she meant you. My stomach flopped. Sorry, what? I squawked. Who?

Her eyes glimmered with pleasure. Gina. Did you ever meet her? Of course, I never thought she was right for him.

For some dumb reason I smiled.

Oh, Franny. She started chewing on a red straw. I don't know what to do. He's so attracted to wounded birds. But he's a good person, really. Just intense. I guess I don't need to tell *you* this, though.

The woman on the street, the bandaged knuckles. *I punched a wall.*

She pointed her red straw at me. But now you've come along, and I say that's a good thing. Don't let any gossip get under your skin, okay? People will judge, people will talk, but fuck them.

Around us the restaurant buzzed with the shrill harsh sound of fun. Oh, I, um. I don't know what Johnny said to you, but I'm actually—

Oh, you're cute. You're adorable. She gave my hand a

squeeze as Johnny slid back into the booth. She's adorable, she told him.

Johnny glanced at her briefly, as if she had lapsed into a foreign tongue. Excuse me. He flagged a passing waiter. Can we have the check?

Oh, already? I frowned. We didn't get to talk about you at all.

We need to go, he said, not looking at me.

~

ON THE SIDEWALK I tried one more time. Johnny, I said.

Franny. He pulled me to him. When he hugged, it was real. Warm, still, steady. A hug I did not know Johnny could give.

We're late, Tess said.

He flicked his hand. The Hodge always starts late.

Tess raised her arm, and a taxi cozied to the curb. Johnny opened the door. Hot sparks pricked my eyes. I had discovered nothing. I would never see him again.

Frances, he said. Just that. Just my name.

9

THE YEAR YOU GOT INJURED, I WAS ACUTELY SENsitive. My breasts hurt, though they still weren't breasts yet, just bottle caps. Simply putting on a shirt was painful, though I liked it, too, and that confused me. This sensitivity spread all over my skin. I wept easily. Other times I could not stop giggling; I would laugh hysterically, sensing that at the bottom of these giggles there were tears. Everything hurt. When the girls talked now in the dressing room, I could hear how much they wanted the boys they loudly disdained; I could sense how badly they wanted clean pirouettes. Their loves and hates bumped up against one another, like boats docked too close in the harbor. It overwhelmed me. Already quiet, in adolescence I tucked further into myself. Creep, the other students began to call me, not because I was a sneak but because they often forgot I was there.

This sensitivity extended to the studio. Now, when the teacher spoke of the proper angle of one's head, when she demonstrated a fouetté or arabesque, I felt it. In my thighs and belly, sympathetic muscles tightened. Slowly, technique unlocked for me. I began to improve.

But though my dancing looked good, I knew it was mimicry. I would never be like you; I was too shy and polite, too careful with my dancing. You were never afraid of mistakes. You weren't afraid to own the stage, demand our gaze, command it with your long legs. Look at me, your body said. Look at me.

At Easter time, you came home with your neck in that brace, talking about going to France, but it was all so vague. I remember you kept saying Johnny wanted to distract you. Distract you from what? I asked, and everyone glared at me.

Your last afternoon at home, we retreated to the attic where we had spent so many hours as children. Dark and creaky, with smudged windows and canted eaves, the attic was our nest, the place where we spun our sister world, where you coached me and did my hair and let me sit for hours at your feet, watching your precise tendus and long balances.

We chatted and stretched, talking idly, until you undid your brace and gingerly turned your neck, a careful owl.

Mom and Dad are worried about you, I said.

Are they?

Yeah. Quitting dance, going so far away. They want you to start college.

Jesus, how did I used to dance in these things?

You had pulled on an old pair of pointe shoes and started bourréeing around the room. I startled; I had thought you were nearly paralyzed.

And what about you? You dropped your heels to the floor and stared at me. Are you worried?

I couldn't help but be a little seduced, as I was whenever you shined your full attention on me. I think you can take care of yourself, I said haughtily.

Good.

Up on your toes again, you pulled off a silky pirouette, flawless, a stretch of satin snapped in the wind.

I stared. Revolving, spinning, spotting with your head: It was impossible.

You can turn.

Oh, I can turn.

I didn't know you were allowed. I mean, I thought your neck—

Yeah, it's basically better. Carelessly you unlaced your shoes. The brace is just—you made quote marks with your hands—an abundance of caution.

It is? Then why aren't you dancing?

It's not the worst thing, taking a break. It gives me a chance to rebuild my technique.

Rebuild your technique, I repeated slowly.

It's a little theatrical, don't you think? Kind of campy?

No. I shook my head. No, no, no. Your dancing is the best thing about the company right now.

I worry I'm turning into a caricature of myself.

What are you talking about? Is that something Johnny says?

Johnny—it's something we agreed I'd work on.

We, I repeated.

We.

Softly I asked, What does he say to you? What does he say about your dancing?

He gives me advice. That's it. It's good advice. He's smart. That review—he said I shouldn't care about that review. He said I shouldn't listen to it. I should listen to him.

Like an insect with soft furry antennae I felt in the air for you, but you withdrew from my searching feelers. I studied your scuttling gaze, sliding sideways. What's happening to you? I wanted to ask. A break from dance? What happened on that island?

Eight years have passed since that Sunday afternoon: the two years you spent traveling, the six in the convent. So of course I wonder whether I'm remembering this right. Maybe you weren't actually doing pirouettes? Maybe you didn't say *rebuild my technique*? I wish you were here, Charley, I wish you could tell me whether I'm getting something wrong, because I feel haunted by this memory. You didn't seem injured. You didn't seem hurt. You pulled off those pirouettes so easily. But if you weren't hurt, why did you run away?

A million times I've asked myself why I didn't push you more. I tell myself I was young, nearly a child, but that's not quite right: I was breaking free of girlhood's chrysalis, I could feel on my skin all the prickles of adult complications. I felt your fear, Charley, and the flap you had fastened over that fear, but I did not draw it back, I did not pick it open, I respected you.

I sighed heavily and stood. Honestly, I can't turn for shit.

Your face brightened. No, really? Wait, let me see.

I laced up my shoes, my pulse fluttering in my neck. Dancing for you made me nervous. After I had wobbled through a double, you nodded knowingly. You've got to think: Push and pull.

Push and pull?

Push the floor away, pull up your retiré. Come on, I'll show you.

Years you had lived in modern's kingdom, but you had lost none of your ballet technique; again and again you cleanly revolved.

I still can't believe you can do that.

Technically, I shouldn't be turning, but— You stopped, panting slightly. Do you see? Push and pull. And you've got to bring your arm *around*. You've got to think—you gestured—*bam*. See? Now you go.

Push and pull. Love and hate. The violence of the foot, the grace of the arm. You showed me how they mixed together, the rhythm of it, and by following your body, putting mine where yours had been, I found it.

A week later you were gone.

10

SOMETHING IN THE WAY HE HAD SAID MY NAME haunted me. There had been recognition in his voice. *Frances.* He had sounded startled, as if until then he had mistaken me for someone else. *Frances.* I replayed the sound of his voice, and decided to give him a call.

As I listened to the telephone ring, I saw myself from above, as if I were watching myself in a movie, as if I were an actress pretending to be an ordinary girl making a pivotal call in her bedroom. I was the ordinary girl, and the actress, and the camera too; I was aware of playing a part. But what part? Still, at that point, I thought of myself as the girl detective, the investigative reporter. Maybe the wounded woman out for revenge.

From the beginning, then, my dealings with Johnny had a touch of the cinematic. To deal with him I had to channel your flair for the dramatic. Your old flair, I should say; I imagine you've given that up, now that you're a nun, but I don't know for sure, and wasn't that a reason I was calling him, too? Because I didn't know my own sister anymore?

Frances?

Startled, I dug my fist into my thigh. I hadn't expected him to pick up. Hastily I launched into the speech I had prepared: Hey, uh, Johnny, I was calling to say it was so nice to see you, but you know, we didn't really get to talk about Charley.

Some static came over the line.

You want to talk about her?

Oh, not like *talk* talk, just like—reminisce, I guess. Does that sound crazy? I want to talk to someone else who knows her. Someone who's not my parents, I mean. I haven't seen her since I was eighteen.

I laughed nervously.

Johnny sounded stern. I don't have any news about her. We haven't been in touch. If that's what you're hoping.

Of course. No, right, of course.

I dug my fist harder into my thigh.

But, umm, do you want to get together again? It's okay if you don't have time. Really, it's okay. I'm sure you're very busy—

No, Frances. He sounded resigned. I have time.

~

STANDING ON THE STEPS of the Metropolitan Museum of Art, I could not stop fiddling with my coat. You know how Mom used to say we should never wear dresses longer than our winter coats, that it was ungainly to let our hems show? A ridiculous, old-fashioned rule, I had thought, but there was something old-fashioned about Johnny that made me remember it now and regret my long dress.

When he came striding up the steps of the museum, I was still yanking at my coat, and I frowned at him before remembering to smile. He looked older in the daylight, his mouth cradled by two saggy parenthetical wrinkles.

Rather than coffee, he had suggested the museum, saying there was an exhibit at the Costume Institute he wanted to see. Inside, he paid the full suggested admission price for both of us. I had never seen a New Yorker do that before, and I laughed aloud; he made me nervous.

Fashion first? He waggled his eyebrows at me.

Blood-spattered kimonos, stacks of mutant suit jackets, explosions of tulle. Dresses like exclamation points and sweaters with three head holes. Steampunk skirts sewn from marigold drapes and leather straps.

Thank you for coming with me, he murmured. I was afraid I was going to miss this.

We had reached a mannequin swaddled in gingham, a hump of cotton growing from its shoulder. Looks like a tumor, I said, pointing. Like cancer.

Are you into it?

I considered, thinking of malignant growth, cells massing in the dark, betrayal in the body. Blue gingham, young Dorothy in Oz, distorted. Yes, I said. It makes me uncomfortable in the best way.

Good. A toothy grin. Me too.

He pivoted. This, though. What do you think of this?

Beside the gingham there was a bridal gown of French lace. Each brocaded rose was exquisitely hand-stitched, every petal veined with silvery-blue thread. Yet this bride had a black veil, and over her shoulders hung leather riding caps, dangling like shorn scalps.

She's carrying the heads of her victims to her groom, I said. She's a serial killer.

He let out a whoop of delight. Yes! She's the executioner. I love it.

The next gown was constructed entirely from white bundles, a demented bride on her laundry day.

And?

I snickered. She's bringing her baggage to the altar. Isn't that pretty much what a wedding is?

Too late, I heard my own words. His face darkened, and he turned away stiffly, his torso a block of ice.

I meant—that came out wrong.

Seems like it came out right.

I was being a cynic.

You're too young for that.

Then all at once he melted. You're right. What is marriage but two people smashing their damage together? He smiled sideways at me. It's not your fault. We're in a room full of wedding dresses, after all. But let's get out of here.

~

RIGHT BEFORE THE LOBBY he stopped at a small gallery's door. Color had returned to his lips; his hands had relaxed.

Quick peek?

Quick peek.

This last room was a little theater. Together in the dark we fumbled past the black curtain to benches covered in carpet. Light shot from the projector.

A memory stirred in me, an early memory of museums and fears.

This video art looked like all video art. There was yellow eye crust, and a man getting punched. Rotting fruit. A razor blade splitting the skin. Two masked men making out. A headless chicken. The flickering sequence, all framed and lit the same, induced in me an odd stupor; I was sucked back to the tedium of childhood, that particular combination of boredom and claustrophobia I associated with watching movies in class.

You okay? Johnny asked.

Yeah.

Intense stuff.

Kind of boring.

A baby's bloody crowning head. The sutures of a stitched wound. A rosy breast leaking milk. That headless chicken again.

It's not even very *good* video art, he whispered.

I began to tell him how my father used to take me to the art museum every Saturday. At first I whispered, but as I described the armor, the impressionists, I grew louder. There was no one else in here, anyway. I told him I liked the room devoted to Duchamp best.

But it also scared me, I said.

I explained how at the far end of this Duchamp room there was a doorway to another room, very dark, with nothing but a massive door on the far wall. It was huge and old, I said, beat-up wood, with rusted screws. Like the door to a dungeon.

In this door there were two holes. You were supposed to go up to the door and look through them. But I never could. I was too scared. Every Saturday we'd spend hours in the museum, and every Saturday we'd end up at that door, and my dad would ask if I wanted to go look, and I would say no.

Excuse me, could you please be quiet? Some of us are trying to watch.

An old man had wandered in. I felt guilty—we hadn't even seen him!—but Johnny laughed as we gathered up our coats, not bothering to duck as he walked through the projector's beam. For an instant frothy water bubbled on his plaid.

In the brightness of the hall, Johnny's eyes drilled into me. So. What happened? Did you ever look?

I nodded. It took me months. And when I finally did, I looked so quickly that my brain couldn't organize what I had seen. I just retained this general sense of humiliation, as if someone had played a trick on me.

So what was it?

It's a diorama. There are woods, and—you don't know it?

Tell me, he said.

There are woods, and a waterfall that moves. It's all shiny. But you don't notice these things right away, because the whole diorama is filled with this very white headless woman, huge, completely out of scale. One arm holds up an oil lamp. And her legs are spread. You can't help it, your eyes go right to her—

But I couldn't say it. When I looked up, his eyes were luminous.

Her—it's so weird. It's this—slit. There's no—

I turned away, pretending to be engrossed in a watercolor of boats. After a moment, Johnny came up behind me. Carefully, he fit his head onto my shoulder, nestling me. His chin was a blunt bone. The warm curl of his ear touched my own.

~

THE EVEN WHITE LIGHTS of the galleries, the hushed conversation, the silent guards, the demented fantastical clothes and swirling video color—all had lulled me into a dreamy associative state where I had started spilling stories from my past, wandering memory's long halls.

But outside in the early winter darkness, the spell dissolved, and Johnny became clear to me again. I remembered what he had done. The image of a door, high and small and blue, through which my sister had disappeared, came to me. She had slipped away, or he had pushed her through.

Doors. I hadn't thought about Duchamp's door in such a long time. Why had I told him such a random memory? I looked over at Johnny walking beside me, his dark hair, his hulk. He was a bank vault, and I was going to break inside.

~

IN THE RESTAURANT, tea lights trembled, and the air was liquid with melting shadows. Greeting Johnny by name, the host took us to a cozy corner table. As if by magic frosted martinis appeared, and then warm bread wrapped in soft cloth, and plump oil-cured olives.

So meaty, said Johnny. Try a red one.

I edged some olive from its pit with my teeth. Good, I allowed. Yeah, meaty.

With the martini it was sublime.

Food arrived, spaghetti nero and radicchio, the pasta briny, the salad dappled purple and cream. Like a gentleman he served me first, but I didn't start right away; I was watching him. With knife and fork he sawed determinedly at a lick of cellulose, the knife clutched loosely in his injured hand. Finally, frustrated, he jabbed, and the lettuce slid off his plate.

Casually, as if nothing had happened, he plucked it up and plopped it into his mouth.

Your bandage is gone, I said.

What?

I pointed. Your hand. Is it better?

He held up his knuckles as if considering them. Yellow dressing shone on his fingertips. Getting there.

You never really said what happened.

No. I didn't.

Do you want to tell me?

He took a swallow of wine. Nope.

Being with him disoriented me. I am sitting across from Johnny Fitcher, I told myself. He is right there. But after so many years of wondering, the whole night had a shimmery vagueness. I was afraid of waking up tomorrow morning with nothing.

Frances, he said slyly. Earth to Frances. What are you thinking about?

I shook my head. Nothing. I honestly didn't think we'd ever see each other again.

He laughed. Yeah, why would we?

Do you mind? You didn't seem very happy to see me that first night.

You took me by surprise.

A beat in which that wild chase down Broadway rose up before me. Jesus Christ. How embarrassing. Gina beside him, a graceful doe.

And then, he continued, when you asked me to drinks—well. It's true that I didn't really want to go. That's why I brought Tess along. For defense, I guess. Sorry about that, I know she's a lot. But I felt I had to have someone else there. Someone else to help gauge your character.

Gauge. As if character could be measured with an instrument.

And? I said.

You're very open, Frances. You drink up everything around you.

I laughed. That's not true.

No. He sounded concerned. I've learned to recognize it in people. A quality of attention. Your sister had it, but you have it more. You're very sensitive.

Charley was pretty sensitive.

Oh, totally. He rolled some bread between his fingers. She would say these things to me after parties that made me realize that even though she was the center of attention, she was also on the side. Watching. But you go even deeper. You pick up on more. I've noticed that.

Wine, a cloud of fruit and spice, prickled my tongue.

You really never talk to her?

He chuckled nastily. I don't think she wants to talk to me. His eyes narrowed. Do you?

No. Well, a card, once a year. But it doesn't say anything. It's like she's dead.

Don't say that.

Nina Simone's voice, haunted, weary, drifted like smoke over the restaurant laughter. Softly I said, Johnny? Can I ask you a question?

Sure.

Did something happen? When she came back from that summer on the island, she was so different.

What do you mean?

Even before the neck stuff started, she was . . . Do you remember that review?

That guy is a jerk. I know him, he's a jerk.

Yeah. But . . . don't you think she was dancing differently?

Frances. If you're asking me a question, then I suggest you ask it.

Was she happy?

Back then? He rubbed his napkin. Look. The truth is that she was dancing better than ever before. She was becoming more nuanced. That's why her injury was so tragic. She was finally getting somewhere.

What do you mean? She was already their star.

Look, obviously, she was already a brilliant dancer. But

she was starting to get bored with coasting on charisma. She wanted to grow as an artist. On the island, we had really started to collaborate. Exchange ideas. I encouraged her. Maybe that critic didn't like the way her dancing was changing, but as I said, that guy's an idiot. She was growing.

And then—she really did get injured?

What do you mean? Of course she got injured.

I frowned. It's so weird, but I have this memory of her doing pirouettes, right before you left for that long trip. She had the neck brace on and everything, but she could spot. She could turn.

Well, she certainly shouldn't have been.

But did you ever think she maybe wasn't as hurt as she said she was?

He puffed out his lips. It's possible. It's possible that she got kind of discouraged. Maybe she was trying to change, but it was harder than she thought. So the injury became a kind of excuse. He slowly nodded. A way to give up before she could fail.

No. She loved to dance. I can't imagine her giving it up.

You didn't really see her in that final year. Hurting her neck really freaked her out. She wasn't as fearless as she used to be.

We both got quiet then, thinking of you. I don't know what memory Johnny called up, but I was remembering those pirouettes, how seamless and silky they were, and then I was remembering being a little girl, wedged in the doorway of your studio, watching you revolve and revolve, fall and get up, skip and hop and try again. Your pink cheeks. The way you bit your lip. How, right before you began, as you pliéd, a look would come into your eyes. Your chin would lift. You'd lock eyes with your reflection. And then off you'd go.

When he began to speak again, it was in a quieter voice.

When she entered the convent—I mean when she cut off contact, and I realized I might not ever see her again—something strange happened. I started talking like her. The borders between us had always been thin, and now I found myself using her expressions. Imitating some of her gestures. It was like she was living through me. For a long time, I felt possessed by her.

Anyway. He splatted flat a lump of bread. I don't know why I'm telling you all this.

I asked you.

No, it's that. He pointed his finger at me. You've got this sensitivity. A deep capacity to feel.

~

ON THE STREET, we found ourselves walking west. The buildings were lit up like birthday cakes, and the air was crisp. Once again I felt as if I were waking up from a spell, as if I had to shake myself awake.

At the light, he threaded his arm through mine.

Shrugging free, I said, Johnny? Can I ask you something else?

Of course. He sounded tired.

What did you tell Tess?

His brow furrowed. I told her who you were. I said you were Charley's sister.

Because she seemed to think—she said something while you were in the bathroom that kind of implied—

Tripping over my words, I flung myself toward the thing not even Tess could say.

Implied what?

I just wondered how you two knew each other.

Oh, we go back a long time.

He stepped into the street and raised his hand. Almost immediately a taxi swerved over. Frances, he said, opening the door for me. It feels so good to be with you.

~

I COULD NOT STAND to pay for a taxi all the way home; I directed the driver to the closest express stop. On the subway platform, I stood there thinking about what Johnny had said. Without exactly believing him, I found that my own memories suddenly seemed hazy. Or no, not hazy: Rather, they had the crisp falseness of film, they had hardened into whatever story my younger self had wanted to tell. Stupidly, it had never occurred to me that the critic could have been wrong, that what had looked like hesitation in your dancing might have been a deliberate softening. And wasn't it like you to push the limits? To ignore the doctor, take off your brace, and pirouette? That wasn't evidence of some ominous change in you. That was a sign you had stayed the same.

A train arrived, and I stepped inside, wondering now whether it had been hyperbole when he said he had begun to speak like you. He didn't sound like you; he sounded like a bear. He didn't move like you; he moved like he was carrying something heavy in an old sack over his shoulder. But still. He had sounded sincere.

~

MUCH LATER THAT NIGHT, I awoke from a dream. Snapping on a lamp, I covered my eyes against the brightness. The apartment, for once, was still. My legs in the sheets looked dull, made from clay, and I pinched them. The dream was already dissolving, falling apart like tissue paper in water, sticking to my hands. What was it? Something about describing the Duchamp diorama, some man saying, No, no, that's not right, you're forgetting—

Slowly I drank a full glass of water, and then sat with my feet on the floor, looking at my hands, my mind going back to those Saturdays with Dad. The endless sterile galleries, that last room of broken glass and a bicycle wheel. Our father encouraging me. Almost pushing me toward the stained wooden door. Go look, Frances. Go take a look. Don't be scared.

And when I had finally looked, at the instant I saw the dull white deadness of her sprawled limbs, I had—

A man. There had been a man. Yes. I had been hovering on tiptoe, peeking through the two little holes, and that's when it happened: a low nasty chuckle. Some man had come into the gallery when my back was turned, some man who knew very well what was behind the door. He had laughed at me. Laughed at the little girl looking at the dirty picture.

Was that true? Did that really happen? I would have sworn it, but ten minutes later I was less sure. Had there really been a man? Or had I only been afraid there might be one? In the window of my bedroom hung the reflection of my face, a yellowish smear. Through the darkness I watched it, floating in the blackness, wondering: Why can't I remember?

11

DAD, REMEMBER WHEN WE USED TO GO TO THE ART museum?

Oh yeah. A chuckle. That was good of me. I was a good father.

A beat. Once again I'd called home spontaneously, thinking I'd tell Dad about seeing Johnny, but when I heard his voice, groaning like the springs of old furniture, I didn't have the heart to agitate him by saying Johnny's name.

Why were you thinking about that, sugar bear?

I don't know. I was trying to remember. Was Charley ever with us?

She always had ballet.

Oh, right.

That was why we started going, actually. I would drive her into the city, drop her off, and then the two of us would go to the museum. Go pick her up at the end of the day. You don't remember?

I was too young.

This is something about being the youngest: Once you're an adult, people forget how little you once were, and how much you missed.

Wasn't I scared to go into that Duchamp room?

What do you mean?

You remember, in the museum, there's that last room, or the last room that we went to, and it was dark, with the big dungeon door, and you would try to get me to look through the peephole?

Oh no, Frances. Dad was laughing. I would've never *urged* you to look through that peephole. That is a very disturbing piece of art. And you were like—seven? No, I never would have done that.

But I remember—

No, you were fascinated. You *wanted* to go look, but you were too little, you couldn't see, I would have had to lift you up, and after I peeked through the hole myself—a little laugh—well, no. I told you you had to wait until you were older. Which was dumb, because then you begged.

No, I was scared.

Maybe you were scared, but you also really wanted to look.

I remember being scared. And then one time I finally did look—

Frances, it's possible, it's very possible. Do you want to talk to your mother?

~

TALKING TO MOM was like bushwhacking through a thicket of brambles, as usual. A barrage of questions pummeled me, and it hardly mattered how I answered them, only that I did so, so that she could get on to the next question.

How are your classes going?

They're good—

And Mira? And what's going on with dance—

Um, dance is good, I actually haven't been going that much—

Did you try that new Pilates place?

I don't really blame her. Losing you broke her. That's a fact. Mom is broken, and nothing I can give her is good enough to make her whole again. Though she did rebuild herself; she did accept that she needed to keep living, but her repairs came out imperfect, her motions twitchy and sped up, as if the only way she could stop herself from sinking down on her bed and never getting up again was to rush through her days like a frantic robot.

I bought my train tickets, she said.

Oh, great. When are you coming up?

And she named a date dangerously close. In truth I'd forgotten entirely about our plan to see the ballet.

Well, honeybun. Anything else?

The automaton rapidly jerks through its mom duties, and then too fast arrives at the end.

Nope. See you soon.

~

WHEN YOU LEFT, Mom and I started going to the ballet. It had become a bittersweet pleasure for me. Watching the saplings who had succeeded where I had failed, who rendered in white pointe shoes the visions of Balanchine, I would sometimes have to look away with a burning throat. In my limbs I could feel every step.

But I went for Mom. She loved it. She would sit in the dark with tears in her eyes, she would grip my hand and squeeze, she would sigh and shout Brava!, this woman who had resisted sending her daughters to ballet, who had sagely predicted that dance would swallow them—now she was lost under its spell. And because I understood this spell too, because I believed, despite myself, in its beauty, I would squeeze her hand back, I would try to put aside my own yearning to be on the stage and rest in the knowledge that we were together, in the dark, dreaming the same dream.

And what dream were we dreaming? Like illicit lovers, we would sit together in that red-and-gold jewel box, not saying your name, not admitting to ourselves what we were doing but, sometimes, weeping.

Inevitably, on the subway, or the next morning at her hotel, she'd wonder aloud whether I *liked* wearing my hair that way, or ask why I wanted to be an English major, poetry and books had never brought my father much joy, why didn't I do something practical instead? Or, in a faux-naive way, she would ask, How are your classes? And then, at my face, she'd add, I'm not asking because I'm nervous you're not going, I'm just asking. And we'd end our visit sniping and regretful. But it didn't matter, not really, because we had the ballet.

Mom: a nervous, agitated woman. In her youth—when we were babies—she had had it in her for a fight, but three-plus decades of marriage to Dad killed that. Now she directed her aggression to petty matters. When I was little she seemed scary; now I mostly pitied her.

This time we had gone to see *Agon*, with two senior soloists who snapped through the Gaillarde, and a baby principal slicing through the famous pas de deux. When she soared on her partner's shoulders across the stage, her legs slowly spreading in a straddle both sexual and like the opening of the Holy Book, I was reminded of you, and the pas de deux that Luciano had first made for you, that erotic duet that had served as your annunciation.

Now I watched as this leggy fawn arched above her partner. Her face blank, her body perfect, she moved within the pentacle of her own anointment, untouchable even when her partner touched her. God, I wanted to be her. I wanted to move like that again.

Then the curtain fell, and I came back to myself. My crunchy knee, my oily face, Mom beside me. Our winter coats, so plain and dull and bulky, marked us as denizens of the ordinary world. My stomach churned. I wanted to do more than clap, clapping was not enough to answer this ballet. I wanted to dance myself. Does that ever go away? Do you still yearn for it, Charley? Tell me, is there ever a time when the beauty doesn't hurt?

As we emerged into the city night, my head ached with longing. The fountain glowed, the poufs of water like white alliums. Slowly we spilled toward it, as if in a dream.

I was thinking we shouldn't linger, I was thinking we should make for the subway, when I saw the man from the Hodge, still with the same precision in his limbs.

Well, hello there, my child.

I could have kept walking, but something in me is stupidly obedient. I stopped, and after a beat so did Mom.

He touched his nonexistent cap. We meet again.

You know this man? Mom asked.

His face in the half-dark had that same grotesque luminosity, the soft plump lips and graying hair, the eyes exaggerated by kohl. We meet again, he repeated. At yet another temple to beauty.

Yes, um, this is my mom—I began to say.

He touched his imaginary cap again—a peculiar tic. Pleased to meet you, he said. Your daughter has good taste in dance. Support her in whatever— He gave a dismissive little wriggle of his fingers. Whatever it is she does.

We do. My mom's voice sounded odd.

Well then. A formal nod. Good night.

Back into the flow of pedestrians he sailed.

Who was that? she demanded.

No one. Just this guy I met once at a show.

Do you know him from school?

Our school employs a lot of weirdos, but not him.

She had her eye on his disappearing back. Is he one of Johnny's friends?

I have no idea.

Now she was looking at me closely. Your father said you've been in touch with Johnny.

Where did he get that from?

You tell me, honeybun.

I *hadn't* told him about running into Johnny on the street, or about Café Lappet or the museum. But Dad likes to exaggerate: I had said *I heard he was back* and he probably turned that into *Frances saw him*. Or maybe Mom had been the one to embellish, maybe Mom had panicked. It didn't matter. Somehow they had gotten my comment confused, and by confusing it—exaggerating it—they had stumbled upon the truth.

I heard he was back in town. That's all.

Well, she said slowly. I guess that's nice. Has he reached out to you?

I don't think he likes me very much.

I'm sure that's not true. She put her hand on my sleeve. Honey? Tell us if you are in touch with him, okay? I think it would be great for you to reconnect, really I do, maybe your father doesn't, but I think it would be a nice thing, but tell us, okay?

I'm not going to be in touch.

We started moving again toward the train. Resolutely I stared ahead, even as I felt Mom's eyes running over my face.

You don't still blame him, do you?

No, of course not.

He didn't make her do anything. It was her choice. I honestly believe it had much more to do with her injury, with trying to deal with the end of her career. But regardless. We have to respect her choice.

Yeah.

Like a surgeon she sliced her card through the turnstile. I know it's hard to understand. Just don't stop talking to us, okay, honey? Keep us in the loop.

12

THE NEXT TIME, JOHNNY WAS THE ONE WHO called, and I wasn't surprised when he did. I had been expecting it, I had even known he would call, not text. Something in his intimacy, his odd formality. I sat down on my bed to answer.

Since the museum a week before, I had thought it over carefully, and what I had decided was this: The memory of a man standing in the doorway to a dark room, that must have been at home, some night when I'd awakened from a bad dream and my father had come to comfort me. When I really thought about it, I could remember him standing in the doorway, his dark body in the lighted square. Somehow the dark room in the museum must have gotten superimposed over my bedroom, the terror of that diorama conflated with my childhood nightmare, everything confused.

Hello? I said.

Frances. You picked up. I wasn't sure if women your age answered the phone.

Well, I saw it was you.

Right.

He said it as if he meant to tease me. Then he coughed. Was I free that Thursday for a show? Two tickets had come his way, comps. He couldn't promise it would be any good.

~

WALKING INTO THE HODGE WITH JOHNNY, past the same ancient usher in her maroon vest and down the sloping center aisle with its nubby carpet, touching the tarnished seat backs and seeing the flickering chandelier, I couldn't stop thinking about that other night with Johnny at the Hodge, that weekend I visited. I couldn't stop seeing you walking between us, glancing back to make sure I was coming, running ahead to catch Johnny's arm. That night of watching you touch him. God, the memories were unbearable. Life was like living in a film reel from which you'd been clumsily excised, leaving behind a fuzzy white outline, a scratch.

Ahead of me Johnny checked the aisle against our printed tickets and began maneuvering down the row. I shimmied after him. When we were both seated, he leaned over and spoke close to my ear.

It meant so much to her that you came that weekend, you know. She always talked about it.

Oh— I startled. That's so weird. I was just thinking about that.

He smiled sadly. Of course you were.

The lights lowered. With a practiced motion Johnny slipped his program onto the floor and rested his hands in his lap. As the curtain rose, he leaned forward and sucked in his breath.

When the overture began, I leaned over. You brought me to *Swan Lake*?

He grinned. You'll see.

Swan Lake's not cool, its gender politics are awful, and not even this hip downtown revamping could obscure the basic cheesiness of the conceit. And yet when the stage silvered and the swans appeared, when that haunting melody began and the long sinuous line of arabesques slowly weaved through the stage, my heart opened. In this production the swans were men and women, goofy and awkward in white feathered suits, but it didn't matter. Beauty hurt. In the dark I pressed each finger against my thigh in the pattern of the piano's part, the notes you taught me to play. Some part of me would never stop wanting to go back. Back to ballet, back to childhood, back to you. I thought of you in your white novice habit, like the white tutu Odette wore, and I wondered whether your gown would turn black, when you would be borne back by your swan sisters, away from the world, away from the prince, deep into the darkness of your enclosure.

~

OUT ON THE STREET Johnny squeezed my shoulder. He had seen the tears I had wiped away.

Dinner?

Once again he did not ask where I wanted to go, and once again I found it deeply relaxing to follow him through the city. As I walked, little swans spun before me. Sometimes he did seem like a prince.

At the door to a candlelit trattoria he hesitated. I used to come here with your sister all the time.

Before I could respond we were through the door and it was all Welcome back, sir! and Good to see you again! and Johnny! My brother! Clasping arms and nodding smiles and curious glances my way.

Once we were seated, he began to talk about animal brides and animal grooms, metaphors of sexual difference handed down through the centuries. He spoke of Odile's deception coming from the tradition of tales in which one bride is substituted for another, and the question of whether love blinds us or allows us to see. As he talked I looked around the restaurant hungrily, at the open kitchen with gleaming copper pots, the hanging baskets and high shelf of wine, the distressed tin ceiling and handsome dark-eyed waiters, and as I looked I was thinking about how I had taken your place, how it should be you listening as Johnny wove a net of art and ideas.

As always, when he got abstract he entered a kind of trance, speaking smoothly while staring at a fixed point on the table, almost as if he were reading the words that slipped so seamlessly from his mouth. Usually so controlled, when he spoke about art he was somehow cut free, a lumbering athlete turned graceful in the pool. Art, ideas, abstraction—these were the lakes in which he loved to swim. Even now he was talking as if articulating clearly the relation between fairy tales and ballet mattered desperately.

I listened politely, telling myself that this was Johnny Fitcher, this was the man you had loved, but when he said *exogamous marriage rites*, I couldn't help it, I laughed.

What? He seemed taken aback.

Nothing, it's just—I feel like I'm in school.

I'm sorry, he said immediately.

No, it's cool, it's interesting. I've never thought about *Swan Lake* like this.

And I smiled, thinking it would please him to hear this. He was a man who liked to play teacher to young women, who felt comfortable reciting familiar knowledge in a singsong voice while someone female nodded.

He pointed at me. Charley used to do that.

Do what?

Smile like that. A little private smile, like some elf had come up and whispered in her ear. He laughed. It was usually when she was thinking something mean. Were you thinking something mean?

No, I said unsteadily, flushing. At least I don't think so. She used to tell you when she was thinking something mean?

Sure, sometimes.

We nudged our plates away.

What kind of things?

Oh, you know.

Things about you?

Yeah, of course. She called me a hack.

At my face he laughed.

Don't look so shocked. We were rough with each other. We tried to be honest. Plus, I had asked.

A hack, I repeated, thinking that this was exactly what Mom had called Dad, back in the bad old days of their fighting.

Yeah, or sentimental, or derivative. All of which might be totally true. I've said them myself.

Practiced hands silently whisked away our plates while others scraped the tablecloth of crumbs. Dessert? asked the waiter, the man who had called Johnny brother, who was—I peeked—wearing the same brand of boot as Johnny.

Some amaro, I think. Whatever you're into these days. Johnny grinned, almost abashedly, and bumped fists. Thanks, man.

When the server had gone, I said, So what did you call her? If she was calling you a hack?

Oh, you know. Nothing much. She could dish it, she didn't really like to take it.

I wrinkled my nose. Charley could take it.

Okay, okay. He laughed. Here's one. She was a complete idiot when it came to directions. That girl could not navigate her way out of a paper bag. This one time she got us totally lost in Paris.

Paris, I said distantly. I remembered the first time she had gone to France. My parents' pleasure; my panic.

We were trying to get to the d'Orsay, he said slowly, letting the word *Orsay* balloon in his mouth. We had tickets, timed tickets, and somehow Charley talked me into taking a city bus, which was a truly terrible idea, but she kept saying, No, no, I've got it, we'll use the map, the map is actually very easy to use. So we're on board, and all of a sudden, she says to me, completely deadpan, That was our stop. So calm. I was like, Are you serious? And she said, Yes, we missed it. Still with that kind of comic detachment.

I laughed. She could be like that. Theatrical. Milking the moment.

I mean, that was the thing. She had no idea where we were, but she was completely chill, and even quite funny about it. Understated wit in the face of calamity.

Was it really calamity?

Oh, no, we still made it. We just had to hike back a bit. But it made me think. In another life she could have been a comedian. She had this kind of sexy reputation but she was actually hilarious.

The word *sexy* from him made me feel funny. Did you get mad at her? I asked.

He laughed. She got mad at *me*.

I mean, did you have a fight? Did you call her an idiot?

Compliments of the chef, said the waiter, sliding down a gold-rimmed dinner plate ringed with raspberries and blackberries, snowy with powdered sugar.

Eat, eat, Johnny urged, pushing the plate toward me. The berries glistened. He took one between his fingers and popped it in his mouth; for an instant I saw it lolling on his pink tongue.

Frances. You're looking horrified. Don't tell me you play nice with your boyfriend. Don't tell me you're not honest with him about his—poems or whatever.

I don't have a boyfriend.

Girlfriend?

Nope.

Smart, he said, cocking his index finger at me. Very smart. Steer clear of commitments right now. Focus on your art.

I don't have an art.

You're a dancer, he said, looking astonished.

I quit.

Oh, sure, you quit. I'm not worried about that. You'll find your way back.

His confidence irritated me. You sound like my father, I told him. I'll be right back.

When I stood, the darkened room of hanging baskets slid around and the light blurred. Unsteadily I grasped my chair's back.

Inside the bathroom it was warm and dark, flickering with candles, filled with a soprano's long trills. My face in my hands, I rubbed my eyes, then my belly.

Slowly, I soaped my hands, peering at my face. At once it hit me: I looked lovely. With a few loose curls, and my jutting collarbone, I was elegant. The booze and heat had put a flush in my cheeks, and my lips were berry dark. Before the mirror I pulled down the neckline to my dress. Then—and I don't know why I did this, I had never done anything like this before—I got out my breasts and pulled on the nipples.

When I returned to the table, Johnny was standing. I've already paid the bill, he said.

Oh, that's good, I said uncertainly.

How long had I been in that bathroom? That dark room of orange and jasmine.

Come on, he said. I've let you drink too much. Let's get you back.

This time when he put me in a cab, I let the driver take me all the way home.

13

AFTER THAT JOHNNY AND I WERE TOGETHER ALL the time. We went to shows, we went to drinks, once we went to lunch. Sometimes we talked about you, but we also discussed dance, my classes, and whatever art he had seen. After a while, we began to talk about his art, too, but he was cagey about it, and I admit that made me jealous: I had the impression he had talked to you quite easily about it. All I knew of his work was those awful sculptures I had seen on Google ten or twelve years ago, but quickly he set me right: No, he hadn't done any sculpture in a long time, he was more into video these days. But he wouldn't describe it.

When we did talk about you, our tone was easy, though there was a little shiver of relief, like the first scratching of an itch, whenever we said your name. I told him how we had played dogs and owners, how I used to follow you around on my hands and knees. I told him the story of your first cigarette, and how you used to cut up your ballet tights, and the way you had screamed at our mother. He told me that the night you two met, you had followed him out of the party and onto the street.

Wait, really? She followed you out?

Oh yeah. He looked embarrassed, pleased, wolfish. From the very beginning there was something electric between us.

In all our stories you were shocking, crazy, an obsessive who carried things too far. Talking about you like this was a relief, though I also knew it was a betrayal. There wasn't the time you had done those pirouettes in the attic, or the bad review; there weren't the long years you had virtually ignored me, or that visit to the feverish sauna. There was only you acting outrageous and capturing our hearts. Every time one of us said, That was like how Charley used to . . . or Did you ever notice how Charley would always . . . , I had the feeling of both entering and leaving my life, leaving the farce called college and entering the room of my childhood, the space of my real self.

Sometimes, though, I worried that talking like this was flattening my memories and reducing you to a series of funny anecdotes. Sometimes, it even seemed to me that we talked about you like you were dead. When I had told Johnny about playing dogs and owners, especially, I'd been aware of something slipping away. I told it as an amusing story, and it was. But it was something else, too, something connected to the bite of carpet, the puckered red skin of my knees. Begging for treats.

Whenever I told Mira I'd been out with Johnny, she said Cool in a voice that made clear it was not. Once she said, What do you do, anyway? You sit around and talk about Charley?

We talk about other stuff.

It's not awkward?

It's nice.

Mira's smell was particularly strong that day, acrid like old coffee, sharpening as she said, I thought you hated him.

He's not as bad as I thought.

She smiled sadly, and after that there was a strain between us, and a compensatory sweetness, a falseness that if I'd been less preoccupied with Johnny would've concerned me more.

But Johnny, and Johnny's stories about you, completely consumed me. I was greedy. He was greedy, too; he loved to talk about you, though sometimes, mid-story, he'd fall abruptly silent. When I looked up, thinking he had lost the thread, I'd find that his eyes were very large, and his hands were scuttling about the table, looking for something to grab.

When that happened I would put my hand over his, and we'd sit like that, quietly, his rough knuckles against my palm.

~

HE HAD A WAY of picking up the check, of looking at it aimlessly, almost contemptuously, before leaning back and tossing down his credit card, that made it seem like it already belonged to him. Once—only once—I had tried to pay, and he had put his hand on my wrist and said, My God, Frances, why?

Since then I had let him. But at the actual slip of credit card, the murmured Thank you, I averted my eyes. It bothered me that I liked it.

I liked it even tonight. We were late for a house concert, which was strange: Johnny hated to be late, especially for performances, and yet he kept dawdling. Shouldn't we get going? I had asked when he ordered another round. No rush, no rush, he had said, and by the time we arrived in Chelsea, the music was over.

The guest of honor, an experimental cellist who had just won a MacArthur, wore a backless dress of gold; she sparkled like the lights and candles, like this whole glassy condo, but when she saw Johnny, her lights dimmed. Well, she said, giving him a one-armed hug. Look who decided to show his mug.

Was she another ex? Who cares, I told myself. So he likes accomplished women. My eye wandered to her cello, plump beside the glossy baby grand.

An older woman in a low-cut cocktail dress came over. Johnnnny, she said, stretching out his name with her big bright mouth. I'm so happy you came.

Of course. We have to toast Analuisa's good news.

Was he speaking more stiffly than usual? The woman lingered, her mouth wide, expecting him to say more. When he didn't, she smiled even wider and said, Where are my manners? Let me take your coats, go get a drink, go eat something, you know Drew insisted on a raw bar, this whole thing is costing a fortune but it's his fortune, so eat, eat!

Usually Johnny was greeted heartily wherever he went, but tonight people dropped their eyes when we approached, their faces went blank, they became abruptly fascinated by their drinks. We darted here and there, bumping into conversational walls, until Johnny steered us to a corner, where we stood shoulder to shoulder, tersely taking sips of pinot gris. What's happening, I wanted to ask, but instead I said, I'm starving.

Really?

Yes, really. We didn't eat, remember? You just kept ordering drinks.

He startled at my directness. Then he smiled. You're right.

I plunged into the party's heart, chasing a tray of spring rolls. But it was strange. Over and over I joined the outskirts of conversational circles, but no one pivoted; no one asked me my name. The women kept looking at me; I kept looking at Johnny, but he was browsing the host's record collection, occasionally picking up an album and furrowing his brow.

Then the thought, deliciously strange: Was I the reason everyone was so cold? Had he broken up with Analuisa recently? Did everyone think I was his new toy?

I began to eat more aggressively: mini quiches and five oysters and a dosa that exploded all over my dress. Finally I drained a flute of champagne and went over. Come on, I said. Let's go.

On the street he dug his chin into his chest. Was that a weird vibe? I asked. Was Analuisa mad we missed the music?

Overrated trendy-ass shit.

But she won a—

He laughed in my face. Then he muttered, I'm so fucking sick of that scene.

~

WE ENDED UP SITTING at the bar in a French bistro where everything was hard and loud and dark. Relentlessly the bartender rattled, the ice smacking against metal as she jerked her silver capsules, as if trying to kill something inside. I studied Johnny. Black hairs burst out from his white skin like snakes; along his jaw, beneath his ear, all over his face, which in the restaurant's low light looked almost blue.

After our food arrived, I said, Is it true that Charley followed you out of a party the night you met?

Johnny retreated behind his eyes without moving a muscle. What made you think of that?

It surprised me.

There are a lot of things that would surprise you about your sister. Taking a big bite of burger, he burst the fried egg with his teeth, and yolk, gold and viscous, spilled over his fingers.

Slowly I said, You're right. There's still so much I don't know about Charley. I feel like I really lost touch with her the summer you were on that island.

Cup. His tone begrudging.

Yeah, Cup. It must have been nice. Being away from everything.

It was. His hands fumbled around the surface of the bar.

Did Charley like it? I asked.

The milky mask returned. She loved it.

What was it like?

What was it like. Oh, Franny. I can tell you what it's like, but I don't know if it will mean anything to you if you haven't been. Sykes House . . .

That's what it's called? Sykes?

Sykes.

I had forgotten the name, if I had ever known it. *Sykes*. I didn't like it; it reminded me of what schoolboys would say right after calling you beautiful. *Sykes.* A promise rescinded, a rug yanked. I tried to focus.

And that was where she decided to change her dancing?

He nodded. Yeah, that's where we decided to work on it.

Did Luciano like it?

Frances! You have this, I mean I like you quite a lot, but you have this sneaky way of approaching a subject without saying what you mean. You're worried I hurt Charley's dancing, aren't you? You're worried I ruined her, and that's why she entered the convent. But Frances, that's absurd. As you said, Charley loved to dance. And I know, believe me, I know, it's very hard to understand the decisions she's made in her life since then. But she's an obsessive. She needs someplace to pour her focus. She's a sucker for discipline. It's really not anything more than that.

Most dancers are suckers for discipline, I observed.

But Charley especially. She's a fiend for it. She—

Excuse me, a woman behind Johnny dingdonged. Excuse me! Yes, excuse me. I ordered a . . .

And the server nodding patiently, and the woman's lips smacking, and her wrinkled hand gesturing. Johnny was still talking, but I couldn't focus on his words, not with the rattle of cocktails being made, and the flopping of the kitchen door swinging, and the conversations smashing in midair, everyone yelling to be heard, every plate filled with slaughtered animals, and the tile, black and white and endlessly repeating, and somehow Johnny was still talking, somehow he was still smacking down his meal and nattering away. For the first time I thought: He doesn't know her. Not like I do.

Eventually we slid from the din out to the gray night. The familiarity of it, walking together in the night after a big meal, helped me calm down. He kept scanning the avenue for cabs, but there were none this far west.

It's fine, I told him. I'll take the subway.

I'll walk you to Eighth.

You don't have to.

I want to.

Quickly the tasteful brightness of Tenth Avenue gave way to a complex of blocky brick buildings sprouting from patchy grass. A dozen times at least I must have walked by these towers, but not until tonight, when Johnny said almost casually that his family had built this complex, did I really see them.

Your family built this?

City contract.

To me the landscape of Manhattan changed the way a riverbank changed, slow or fast but completely beyond the control of us creatures scurrying in shadow. That Johnny could look at a building and think *We did this* astonished me. Beside me he seemed to grow older and larger, made of brick and stone himself.

Yep, Johnny was saying, glancing up at the towers. We still manage them too.

They're . . . public housing?

Yeah. All the city vouchers, there's actually money in it.

I craned my neck up. From many windows hung AC units, precariously held in the jaws of black frames. On one floor, the lights were out, and the red EXIT sign made a bloody disco of the hall.

Of course, Johnny said, following my gaze, sometimes that profit depends on being, erm, judicious in your maintenance.

The terror of walking through a dark hall. I could feel it, could imagine a small child's hand in mine; could imagine myself as that small child, the hallway moving with shadows.

Can't you say something? I asked. Make them take care of it?

Make who? He turned, his lips wet.

Your dad? Or the—company, or whatever?

Fitcher Realty does what it pleases.

But don't you—I mean, it's yours, right?

Yes and no.

How could it be, I wondered, that in all our family's talk about Johnny's wealth we had never once asked about the exact structure of it? Real estate, you had said, and we had all accepted it; we hadn't thought to ask anything more.

I remembered how Professor Chalmers had talked of Rochester's wealth, his time in the sugar colonies, how

Thornfield Hall was built with enslaved labor and blood, and how Bertha, the first bride, the Creole bride, rambling through the upper halls, was the ghost, the ghastly reminder of this sin. I thought of this, and then I thought the towers were something different; and then I thought again that I wasn't entirely sure.

We had reached the corner. Johnny's face was again that milk-white mask. Does your family own a lot of public housing? I asked tentatively.

They own a lot of everything. He blew some hair from his face. Look. I have to tell you something.

What?

And he looked so sad that I wanted nothing but to comfort him; without my even deciding, my face fell into a pose of sympathetic understanding. Why did I do this? I don't know; it's something in me, something that wants to soothe, to make nice; maybe it's in all women like me.

I wanted to say that spending time with you has been deeply meaningful to me.

Okay. We had left the towers behind us and were walking under new lights.

I'm going to go away for a while.

You are?

Gray brown and pitted, the sidewalk folded into hills.

I'm—I'm encountering once again the ways in which events have grown bigger than my capacity to absorb them.

Oh.

I'm feeling pretty sad and scared.

Yeah, I said quietly.

I don't recognize myself in the stories that people are telling about me. It's very disorienting. I need to go away for a while.

Okay. Where will you go?

Probably to Cup. I don't know, Franny. I can't get into it all. The world feels too raw and painful to share.

Yeah, sure. I get it.

I looked up. His eyes were bright.

Still he didn't move. Still he was looking at me. A grain of unease. His eyes were so big and luminous. Then he nodded, strangely formal and stiff.

When I got home I took a long hot shower, scalding myself until the back of my neck was blotchy and red.

14

WITH JOHNNY GONE, I DIDN'T HAVE A WAY TO hold on to you anymore. I had grown dependent on him; I could no longer talk to you on my own. It felt flat. I found myself browsing the Fiore Dance website and clicking through the bios of their dancers, which was how I discovered that Luciano, probably in a bid to make money, had started offering classes for adults.

Since that undergraduate ballet class, embarrassingly easy, I had sworn off dance, but as I clicked on the schedule, as I noted the times and the price, I realized I was going to go. That very afternoon, as if entranced, I changed into my old dance clothes and rode the subway downtown.

When I entered the studio (the one on the top floor, where you must have spent so many hours), I was afraid of the fuss if I were recognized as your sister, but it quickly became clear I didn't have to worry. Etai, the teacher, was my age; he must have joined the company long after you left, and he barely glanced at me when I nodded hello.

No, he had other business at hand. Long and thin, like

a stick with its leaves stripped, he stood in the center of the room and commanded, Float.

Slowly the others trailed their arms, rippling their torsos like drifting seaweed. Flailing, I did my best to follow.

Then I saw him. It shouldn't have surprised me. Even in New York the dance world is small, and the downtown dance scene even smaller, so the fact that the girlish man from the Hodge was there was not exactly shocking. But still. I was surprised.

Discreetly I placed myself a few feet from him and began to do my own gyrations. If he recognized me, he gave no acknowledgment. In his black nylon pants and waffle shirt, he looked older, more definitively male, with a concave chest and gray hairs furring his neckline. Tired eyes. A halo of empty space surrounded him; I could practically hear the other girls wondering if he was a pervert. Though these were in theory open classes, available to anyone, everyone besides Etai and him was young and female, perky ex-dancers with ponytails. The trickster from the Hodge, with his aging male body, dropped the temperature of the room.

But only so much, for class is ritual, and ritual is repetition. Etai spoke in a clear, low voice, a wizard casting his spell.

Find the weight of your bones. Measure their weight.

Sumptuously we carved circles with our hips, we caressed the air with rippling legs. My spine slithered, my feet discovered articulation.

Drop into your weakness, Etai intoned. Find your loose flesh. Your happy flesh.

We sagged, we drooped, we shook. It felt good, bad, funny—at any rate, strange—to move in this way. Like you.

Measure the weight of your wrists, your rib cage, your toes.

Our wizard looked pale and empty, with purple half rings beneath his large-lidded eyes. I can remember you looking like that. Hollowed and flaming, as if a virus were consuming you from the inside. The virus was dance. Dance eats you up, it gobbles your youth, it swallows everything. And I trembled as I danced; and I thought that I was glad that I had escaped, even though it made me ache.

Draw with the top of your head, Etai said. Draw with your fingertips. Chew gum. No, *chew gum*, stretch out your mouth, your eyes. Chew gum with your stomach. Chomp.

I tried, I really did, but it was no good, I could not lose myself. I was afraid of letting go with that man around, I kept looking over at him. Twisting, folding, he unwound his arms, he circled like a mobile, he fluttered like wind chimes. That he had once been a serious dancer was evident in every tilt of his shoulder and hip; that he was much diminished was evident too. I kept trying to catch his eye, but no matter how often I glanced over, he was lost in himself.

After class, as he chatted with Etai, I laced and unlaced my shoes, lingering, gaming my exit so that we'd end up together by the elevator. It worked. As I approached he bowed his head, grinning; I had the idea he was aware of my subterfuge. Well, hello there.

Hello, I repeated idiotically, staring at the fat smudge of pancake foundation by his temple.

Good class. He jerked his head in the direction of the studio. He's got his way, building you up. Almost reminds me of Luciano's class back in the day.

Oh, did you dance with—

The elevator dinged, and we stepped inside. A little tick as the machine began to move.

He snapped his fingers. Did you ever find your Johnny Fitcher? You were looking for him.

What? Oh, yeah. Yeah, I did.

Good. He nodded curtly, as if I had completed some assigned task. Desperately I tried to think how to keep the conversation going, but then the elevator dinged again and the door gaped open and he was striding away.

I caught him at the exit. Do you really know Johnny?

Holding the door for me, he sighed. Nothing can help him now, isn't that right?

Nothing can . . . ?

You haven't heard? Well. He fluttered his hand. It's a trifle. Tempests and teapots and all that. Good night, my dear.

Wait.

He stopped, still holding the door.

Um, ah. I'm Frances, by the way.

He gave another one of his formal nods. Paul.

The receptionist muttered, Close the freaking door, and guiltily we did, stepping out together into the street.

What do you mean? I asked. What's going on with Johnny?

Night had fallen while we had been dancing; a few commuters hurried past, bent at the shoulders. I zipped my jacket and turned up the collar. He narrowed his eyes.

Frances. Frances Garbinski, would it be, by any chance?

I nodded.

Paul Sonette. He held out his hand. I danced with your sister a long time ago.

As I shook his hand I realized some part of me had recognized him from our first meeting, some part of me had known he was the older man with whom you had danced your first pas de deux, you in the pale bikini, he barechested and grasping, that fur on his chest, his lips so plump and feminine.

I should have known, he was saying. You look so much like her.

I looked down at my feet. She's taller.

She's a lot of things.

Without discussion we started drifting east together. What's going on with Johnny? I said. Please tell me. He's totally stopped speaking to my family.

This was admittedly a little dishonest of me, but it was worth it when Paul sighed and said, Will you get a cup of coffee with me?

We walked to a well-known coffee shop whose barista was pulling down the metal grate, and another where a sad boy was slinging a mop beneath overturned chairs.

Hmm, Paul said, casting his glance up and down the block.

I shivered in my thin jacket.

Hmm. We could get a drink, except you don't look old enough, and entirely inconveniently I stopped drinking a long time ago. Hmm, my dear. Should we go to my place? It's two blocks from here.

To your house? I squeaked.

To my house. I know, terrifying. But I'm harmless, I promise. And this morning I got a fresh packet of the most marvelous gunpowder green tea.

I'd love to, I interrupted him.

As we walked it struck me that I'd spent months with Johnny and yet never been near his place, but all at once and quite easily Paul was inviting me to his. The invitation had startled me, but I wasn't scared of him. Away from the other girls, especially, it was even more obvious how—not harmless, I wouldn't say, not sexless, but how *witchy* he was. A good witch. He was going to tell me something significant about you. I could feel it.

Here we go, he said, leading me down a cement stair to a garden apartment on a brownstone block.

Inside all was red plush, lace over lamps and dark old wood, thrift shop paintings of sour-looking boys and framed programs from long ago. A musty smell, a thin Oriental rug, worn in patches. So the retired dancer burrows into genteel poverty, I thought. Cast aside, he lives on the margins of his art, memories boxed behind glass. No wonder you latched on to Johnny; no wonder you wanted a different fate.

Paul made us a pot of tea and handed me a thin china cup before sinking into a leather recliner that farted softly with escaping air. Seated, he changed again: No longer a puppet or doll, he reminded me now of a lion, with his broad shoulders, lined face, and the snow in his hair. Regal. How quickly he could change. This liquidity must have been what drew Luciano to him, this slippery shape-shifting quality. I tried to remember more about the pas de deux.

When I noticed Paul looking at me expectantly, I tensed, thinking how to begin, but before I could ask anything, he started speaking.

Johnny's got good taste in women.

He took a slurp from his cup.

I'll give him that. He's got good taste in *art*, everyone knows that, and he doesn't mind when a woman is more successful than he is. In fact he likes it. He knows his main job is to dole out the money, and he's a good sport about it.

But people don't like him?

Well, there's a funny thing about Johnny. He seems to have an almost psychic sense of when someone is going to be successful. I mean the women he dates, he finds them, and then their careers blow up. They get famous. Not like *famous* famous, but they become—prominent, let's say, in their fields. And then—

And then?

It's never his fault. It's never anything he does. But they seem to . . . well, like with your sister. She got hurt. It's fine. Lots of dancers get hurt. Injuries are a part of life. But—

But—

It's hard to say. Basically, the women, they stop making art. There was this painter, Krista, right after your sister. She cheated on her wife to be with Johnny, and when the wife found out, she asked for a divorce. It got acrimonious, it ruined Krista financially, and she had to give up her studio space. Not exactly Johnny's fault, but still, the fact is, she doesn't paint anymore. Or with Tess. Johnny convinced her that she was a better editor than writer, that she was wasting her time writing fiction, and it's true that now she's an enormously successful editor, she's had a tremendous career. But there does seem to be a pattern.

You think it's his fault.

Holding the teapot high, he poured more mossy liquid into my cup. Some sloshed onto the saucer.

Did you know that Luciano wanted to revive *Bluebeard*?

Bluebeard?

The dance. Her debut. He gave her the pas de deux.

That you danced with her. I almost whispered the words.

Exactly. He wanted to revive it, that last fall. I think he hoped it would help with her confidence. They started to rehearse it too. And I don't know, this is all hearsay—I had retired by then—but I heard she wouldn't do it.

Wouldn't do the dance?

Wouldn't do the—do you remember?

He brought his hands flat together and slowly hinged them wide, the way a child might mime a dove, except his hands weren't meant to be wings, they were legs, my sister's legs, how they had split wide at the center of the stage.

She wouldn't do it anymore. She said it made her uncomfortable. She wanted him to change the step.

I didn't believe it. You were always the bold one, Charley. You were never inhibited or afraid. You made sex seem like a joke, a fact of life, not worth the big fuss; you were comfortable with bodies, yours and others', and you respected the choreographer. Refusing to do a step? No.

Seeing the skepticism on my face, Paul smiled. I know, I know. Luciano was shocked too. Apparently they had a huge fight. And then—that was it for Luciano. Once a dancer doesn't trust him anymore, once she won't give her body to him—it's over.

What do you mean, it's over?

He stopped casting her.

I thought she got injured.

He shrugged. He gave her small parts. That started even before the trouble with her neck.

I closed my eyes, sympathy flaring within me. Falling out of favor with the director. That was something I could understand.

But what about now? I asked. What's going on with Johnny? Why is everyone mad?

My dear, it's not mine to tell. But you're a smart girl. You already know it, if you have the courage to look.

At the end of that pas de deux, you sat slumped against the wall. Paul came up and yanked you by your feet. You were jerked forward; the back of your head hit the floor. With a snap, you shoved yourself back. Again he yanked; again you shoved. Over and over. Violent, unceasing, woman and man. Repulsive.

Now there was some of that same abruptness in the way Paul pulled me to him. I stiffened. He squeezed my shoulders between his arms, strong and rigid as he smacked my forehead with a kiss. Quickly I wiped it away. He watched me with that same sardonic smile, those same yellow teeth.

I really should have known you were her sister. The resemblance is striking.

A gray cat with yellow eyes suddenly appeared, rubbing itself against the piano legs. I shuddered.

Kitty kitty, called Paul.

I wound my scarf around my neck. Paul, I said. Was my sister happy? Did she like dancing for Luciano?

She liked it more than anything in the world.

And with Johnny?

I had left the company by then. He shook his head. I really don't know.

15

CHINATOWN. SCRAWLED SILVER OBSCENITIES ON rooftops, a line of white laundry. I walked alone over the bridge, thinking about the women, waiting for it all to cohere into sense. The Brooklyn Bridge, with her graceful wires, soared beside me, gray and pale, a shimmering question, a chimera. Usually I chose her, the pretty bridge, but today I hadn't wanted beauty; I wanted ugliness, the chest rumble of rattling trains, the heaps of gray-black trash, fossilized like hills. I breathed dirt and thought about Johnny's hand sliding up your leg. Your laughter in the bar, your song. Black hair, thick and curled, beneath his cuff. Oil slicks on the water. The shocking rank smell of sweat and sleep. The light under the door. The light across the water.

What had Johnny done to you? What had he done to Gina, to Krista, to Analuisa, to all these women with names that ended in soft sighs, so that when I called them it sounded like I was moaning? I had heard Johnny call them, and I had seen them, these women so beautiful I could not close my lips when I named them. But I named them now.

Down below, a tiny carousel, safe in a glass box. The water too white to gaze upon directly. Our cocktails of citrine and rose, the pasta black and briny. The bathroom, papered in plum and onyx, with a candle that smelled of orange blossom. Nina's smoky voice. Studying my face, my abruptly lovely face, my long slender neck, my eyes that were your eyes. My hands at the neckline of my dress, my hands pulling at my breasts.

When at last I reached the jumbled confusion of Downtown Brooklyn, I had all the off-ramps and traffic lights and plazas of a city but no coherence, no logic, no sense. I blew my nose, and the tissue turned black. Smog: That was what the bridge had given me. Dirty air.

~

THE PARTY WAS HELD DEEP in Brooklyn. I went there alone, on a grim subway train that heaved and sighed over trash-strewn tracks, and when I knocked on Ben's beat-up door, no one answered. I checked the address again and then tried the knob. It turned.

Inside, the quintessential bachelor living room: leather couch and huge TV. Uneasily I walked back, following the sound of party chatter. In the kitchen, a few girls were sitting on countertops, drinking whiskey and swinging their legs. They ignored me as I scooted for the screen door.

Green and glittery, the yard seethed with shouting, laughing, drinking, a fervid hum. I stood for a long moment on the cement stoop, watching. It was unseasonably warm for April, and the long blue evening was a fairy-tale enchantment, the boys in cotton T-shirts so thin I wanted to press my palm against them. A grill was going, two boxes of pizza sprawled open on the picnic table, there were tiki torches and cigarettes and a votive candle flickering. A majestic mulberry tree, viridian and berry black, sprawled over it all, a canopy of green slung with silver Christmas lights.

I didn't belong. Everyone was older than me, more gorgeous than me, with laughing eyes and ready quips. If Mira hadn't rushed up to me right then and wrapped her fingers round my arm, I might have fled.

But there she was, exclaiming, Girl, thank God. To her uniform of black cardigan and black jeans she had added dark eyeliner and chalky red lips, and that was how I knew she was nervous, even before she said, You won't believe who's here. *Her.*

Before Mira, Ben had dated a woman who played in a band, a sparkling impetuous pixie who had taught him how painful desire could be. Turned me into a Buddhist, he apparently liked to say.

He actually invited her?

She's performing. Mira swayed. I'm totally fucked.

You're not fucked.

I am. I could die. I could just die.

The air that night had bite. Conversation flashed like little knives; the laughter was cruel. There were a lot of poets around. Poets finishing novels had been "thinking a lot about John Ashbery lately." Poets behind on their dissertations had been "fucking around on GarageBand." Poets who had founded poetry presses were lifting weights; poets with rich parents had been "working upstate." Beneath their words I heard everything. I knew their nervous hearts, their loving mothers. Not only the poets, either. Party girl Buddhists had given up their pill addictions, and vegan Buddhists in soft cotton wanted to waft away. To a small adoring circle, a grad student imitated Harold Bloom's booming sonorous voice:

Now, children, what is God?

At the uproarious laughter, he flushed pink, and I saw the seven-year-old boy in his thick glasses, praised by the teacher for his book report.

Ben's ex played in a band called Petit Pouce, so of course Petite Pussy had been the joke all night, guy after guy saying it. Pouce, the girls would snap, and one even fished out her phone. It means thumb, she reported. They're Tiny Thumb, jackass. And everyone laughed.

Would Johnny think that funny? Probably not. He wouldn't have had to look up the French, either. He wouldn't think these poets were adults; he probably wouldn't even call them poets unless they had a book or two. No, he'd sniff and call them babies; he would call this party young and dumb. Alone at this party I was young, maybe the youngest one here along with Mira, but with Johnny in my mind I could be old and judgmental. When I thought, They're childish, it was his voice speaking through me.

At my elbow Mira said, Oh shit. They're about to play.

I could smell her, her characteristic stale odor, subtle but pervasive, a smell I strangely loved. Her lipstick had smeared and I dabbed her mouth; she shrugged me off.

The poets quieted. Two white girls, one in a trashy turquoise ball gown and the other in something tight and black, with flowers tatted up her calf, began to drone. Their voices, high and haunted, summoned Nico, the seventies, the Factory, Warhol. But threaded with white-hot pain.

Mira nodded at the girl in black. That's her.

She looks like a ferret, I said, but I was lying. She was gorgeous, and she was talented: With her bandmate she slipped between half a dozen instruments, handing off guitars and bass, tapping out a few notes on the keyboard, keeping up her wordless keening.

Behind them on a brick wall played a projected video. In grainy footage it showed the same two women in matching bridal gowns, at matching drum sets, robotically drumming. Their faces, with a trick of editing, had been replaced with skulls. Under their lace veils, dark holes for eyes.

The effect was hypnotic: skeleton brides at their drums, live women in black and green, varied and strange, now with a bass, now with a flute. No one could look away. The brick wall sprouting moss, the mulberry tree strung with lights, the soft gray sky, city-close, starless. Magic. When they finished, everyone clapped and whooped. The women smiled shyly and said, Thank you, we are Petit Pouce, thank you.

I squeezed Mira's arm, and she squeezed back.

After that the party got strange. I found myself with a beer bottle in my hand. The lip of the neck felt sexual against my tongue. A white dog trotted through the party. Somewhere an owl hooted. The dog snapped at a pizza slice and a girl burst into tears. Someone named Pony introduced me to a circle of boys discussing megafauna. Then Mira was back at my elbow, whispering, Help.

I pivoted from the laughing boys.

Ben's disappeared.

Automatically my eyes flicked around the party. A sea of mouths, and the white dog was loose again. Overhead the mulberry loomed, branches spread like fingers over a face.

And the girl, Mira added. Petite Pussy.

We'll find them, I said.

Holding hands, we pushed through the party. Nobody stopped us as we opened the door to the kitchen, nobody stopped us as we walked down the hall, throwing open bedroom and bathroom doors. There was no one. Not even a small circle with white powder and a mirror, not even a couple making out on top of coats. Nothing.

Mira wrinkled her brow. Let's try outside.

We found them on the street, outside the glow of porch light, not kissing or even touching but standing like they might: Ben leaning against a street post, Ms. Pouce canting her hip and pouting up at him.

Mira swore and spun on her heel.

At the slammed door they turned. My eye met Ben's. His vapid, clear blue eyes. You suck, I muttered. You fucking suck.

Frances, he started to say, and I too spun on my heel. Behind me I could hear him cursing. Some Buddhist.

I found Mira in one of the bedrooms, standing at a dresser, pinching between her thumb and forefinger the wire hook of an earring. This is hers. She spoke blankly. I know it.

I glanced around the room at the navy-blue bedspread, the ochre meditation pillow, the mandala on the wall, and the book *What the Buddha Taught* on the nightstand.

Maybe he let her get ready in here?

She let out a snarl, and I thought she might cry, Mira who was as dry and papery as a fallen leaf, Mira who in her low reedy voice was always explaining calmly why it made sense to continue with Ben—briefly I thought her armored reasoning had been chinked.

But she recovered herself. She sat on the bed, feathered earring in her hand, and said, I hate him.

Good. You should.

I hate him.

And there they were: tears. Her face shattered, a gasp erupted from her depths, and she threw herself on the bed and sobbed.

Tentatively I reached out and touched her shoulder. From beneath her hair she said, I'm going to give him up.

Okay. Okay, good.

I stroked her back in timid circles.

I'm going to, I'm going to tell him—she turned her red squished face to me—that we can't see each other anymore. That it's not—worth it.

He puts you through so much.

Yeah. Her face crumpled, and I tucked back her hair. Yeah.

For a long time I rubbed her back. Eventually her sobs quieted, and her breathing lost its jagged edge. But even after she had fallen asleep I continued to pat her, staring vacantly into space, thinking of the Buddhist and his desires and his old love. An ex, not reduced to a shell but alive and vibrant and very close: the other possibility that the new woman fears.

From the hall came the sounds of cooing goodbyes and clomping shoes. I kept expecting Ben to return, but he never did. Beneath my hand Mira was gently snoring. The smell of his bed must comfort her, even now.

When the floodlights from the backyard flicked off, I shook her shoulder, whispering, Mira.

Like a child she blinked open her eyes; like a child she rose and stretched, sat docilely on the bed while I gathered up our shoes and sweaters and led her to the door.

~

ON THE STREET the temperature had dropped, and a paper cup traced two circles as it spun, the waxy weighted bottom anchoring its swinging lip. Towers the color of wet sand leaned crazily. A police cruiser crawled past.

After crying, Mira seemed even more withdrawn. In silence we walked alongside a boxy park ribbed with pointy black fence. Beyond the fence a woman in sweats drowsily paced behind a corgi, and I thought of the little white ghost dog threading happily through the party, begging for scraps, content and free.

How's Johnny? Mira asked.

Johnny, I said wonderingly. I don't know. He's out of town.

Mira snorted. Ran away, huh?

Yeah, actually. I did feel like he was running away. But I don't know why.

She looked over. You really don't know?

All at once I thought my chest might explode. No. Did something happen?

Right. Of course. Why would he tell you? Hold on. She slung out her phone, dabbed and tapped, then held out the screen. So you haven't seen this?

I winced at the brightness. What is it?

Read.

~

THIS PARTICULAR POST HAS BEEN DELETED, but it doesn't matter, you've read a hundred like it. You know the high-minded start, the tone of persecuted outrage, the flares of sarcasm and dark insinuations. Even I found my eyes glazing over, though when I saw her name, my heart dropped, and I saw again her face: the porcelain skin framed by the black bob, the tiny hooflike boots picking through the February slush, her laughing winking irony as she watched Johnny try to squirm out of drinks with me. Gina.

Accompanied by a moody black-and-white portrait of herself, her post apologized for her silence *here* before explaining that she was now getting the help she needed to recover from a relationship she hadn't recognized as abusive until too late. A *prominent funder of the arts* had bullied and gaslighted her, criticized her clothing and her hair, punched the wall near her head, and even—she had discovered—held on to compromising video she had never wanted him to take. Now, she told us, she was scared. Scared of what he would do. But she wouldn't be governed by her fear. No, she was writing today to warn other women. She would not be silenced. She had a voice.

Oh, I said. Oh.

Mira raised her eyebrow.

I looked down again at Gina's list: insomnia and anxiety, struggles with self-worth, difficulties at work . . .

That night at Café Lappet: *I punched a wall.*

That afternoon with Charley: *It's something we agreed I'd work on.*

That morning of the wedding: my father red with rage.

All those phone calls home, all those dark glances my parents exchanged. My father's wary insistence that I leave Johnny alone.

The whole ride back to Manhattan Mira and I didn't speak, but after Canal, I rested my head on her shoulder, and I knew we were both thinking of skeleton girls, drumming in bridal gowns.

~

LEARNING THE TRUTH about Johnny broke the spell. His crime became specific, therefore containable. My mind had particulars to imagine, and for a while I did imagine them: the angry shouts, the snide comments, the thrown punch.

For a few weeks I kept tabs on Gina's post, but after the first sympathetic burst of comments, there was no traction, no other women coming forward with stories of their own. The Hodge removed Johnny's name from their list of donors. But if there were more repercussions, I couldn't tell.

Then came a period in which not much happened at all.

Sometimes life is like that: fallow. Not good, not bad. Or rather, good and bad in such equally trivial measures that it's not worth remarking upon. Life just bumps along, a toy train clinking over plastic tracks. How are you doing? Mira would ask, and up from my mind would rise a perfect blank. Fine, I'd say uncertainly. Good? Yeah, things are okay.

You never said that you were "fine," life never clinked along for you, things were never simply "okay," they were always complicated, shifting, transforming: Something was always being born, something was always dying. Life never stopped. Even as a kid I had noticed this tendency of yours to put yourself in the middle of a big dramatic story, centering yourself in a swirl of magic and upheaval. I had envied it. Even now I sometimes wondered whether my failure to see myself as the protagonist of my own life story had something to do with growing up in the shadow of such a *character*.

Now I told myself I was in a story where my sister's evil ex-husband was revealed to the world as evil. He had been unmasked, disgraced, and sent away into exile. But the thought didn't satisfy me. It was not enough. You were still in France, kneeling before your narrow bed, or singing Ave Marias with ancient Frenchwomen. (Forgive me, I have nothing with which to picture your new life, I have to illustrate it with cliché.) You were still deciding whether to give yourself away.

A fallow period: sure. But inside, an urgency. Seven springs ago you entered the convent. Soon you might take your vows and disappear behind those walls forever. And I still didn't know why. Maybe Gina exaggerated, maybe Paul liked to gossip. Maybe the critic was wrong, maybe your injury really had been severe. Maybe Christianity filled you the way dance once did. Or maybe not. Conjecture satisfied me less and less.

16

THE SUNLIGHT THROUGH THE DIRTY GLASS WARMED me, at first pleasantly and then, as the delay dragged on, oppressively, my face growing flushed and hot. The smell of the train thickened with breath and body odor, someone's bologna sandwich, and when I tired of looking out the window at the woods, I watched the flicker of disgust on the faces of people as they entered our car.

It had snowed the weekend after Johnny left, a heavy wet spring snowstorm that left slush in the streets and gutters running with bright water, but after that it had gotten steadily warmer, the late April days touching eighty, all the city's dogwoods and magnolias blooming and then dropping their blossoms together, so the city was again full of snow, before the flowers turned brown and scummy underfoot.

On the first Tuesday in May, with two weeks left in the semester, I had sat in The Brontë Sisters with my fingers itching. When class ended I'd counted to ten. Then I stood and stretched before pushing my chair squarely beneath the seminar table. As I walked to the elevator bank, blue electricity licked my calves. In my hand my phone was hard and warm.

From the stoop of a brownstone I dialed. A silver rod plunged from my throat to my belly when he answered.

Frances? I was just thinking about you.

His voice was relaxed and warm. The silver rod flattened into a giant mahogany wing.

Really?

Really.

A bloom of silence between us, thick and petaled, redolent and still.

I've been doing some spring cleaning, up here at the house. Going through old boxes. I found something that used to belong to your sister.

Really?

I want you to see it, Frances.

And there it was again, the way he said my name. My name, so different from yours, so old-fashioned, though I could have copied you, gone by Frankie or even Frank, followed you into fleet tomboy sexiness—but I had not, and I heard in the way he said my name that he understood why not. He pronounced all the softness inside those syllables, their aching corners.

~

WHERE IS THIS PLACE? Mira had kept asking. Where is it exactly?

It's an island.

And I'd point again at the map on my phone.

I've never heard of it.

It's very small.

Why do you have to go?

I told you, he invited me. He says he has something for me.

Okay, okay. She'd nod squarely at the wall, playing the part of the hero in an old Western, stonily contemplating the long odds. I'd take the opportunity to slip another shirt or dress into my old duffel, but when she looked over, I was ready.

But why the whole weekend? Couldn't you go for the day?

It's a long trip. And Mira. I feel like this is where things started to go wrong for Charley. I want to see it.

Okay, okay, I get it. She held up her hands. It's a kind of pilgrimage. Just be careful.

~

IN THE FERRY OFFICE a man with a weathered face and a knitted cap looked at me so hard I thought he might refuse to sell me a ticket. But finally he said, Round trip?

Round trip.

Well then. He nodded at the clock. You've got two minutes.

I ran. I made it, and once on board clambered up to the deck. I was alone, and darkness had fallen. Around me, men in blue windbreakers stamped CREW tied off ropes, their radios squawking. Below, the ocean was an inky oil spill. The motor throbbed beneath my feet.

Then: the bowel-loosening blare of a foghorn. We were off. I watched the wooden dock get smaller and smaller, thinking now I had truly done it. There was the thrilling smell of gasoline, and salt from the sea; there were great handfuls of stars, white light flung carelessly against the blue-black curtain of sky, and cream-colored caps on the water.

Soon a few other passengers joined me. They all looked like paper cutouts from magazines, the men in chinos and boat shoes, standing on deck with beers in hand, laughing tight hard laughs. Their wives had complicated faces. They had done so much to smooth and spackle, but the violence of the years was still smashing through in spidery cracks. They wore navy shifts or bold floral prints, and had ashy blond hair, pearl earrings, pale pink nails, and tasteful lipstick.

There were also some teenagers with long gawky limbs, and men my age smoking cigarettes and talking out of the corners of their mouths. Together we took in the departing shore, but when we reached open water and the wind began whipping, most everyone descended below. I stayed above, watching the red buoys bobbing. All around me the sound spread, the color of dull metal, and if I had a thought in my head it was simply this: I was going to find some answers.

The sky darkened, and the water turned the color of smoke.

As we approached the island, I could make out the shape of houses amid the trees. No lights. When we docked, I was alone on the upper deck, shivering. The crew spun around me. Down below, all the preppy couples had returned to their cars. I squinted. The island was an empty parking lot fuzzed in fog. Smells of sea funk and gasoline.

I spotted Johnny leaning against a small blue truck, arms crossed. When he saw me he grinned, teeth white in his new beard.

That beard. Not huge, neatly groomed, yet somehow it resembled black vegetation swallowing his face.

I stepped into his waiting arms and remembered how good he was at hugging. His embrace solid and square. Honest, I would have said. Bristly beard scratched my cheek.

He pulled back. You came. I didn't think you'd really come.

I dinged his beard. This is nice.

Ah yes. I'm going feral.

By now the last of the cars were leaving the ferry, their headlights sweeping over us in a regular white rhythm. He swung my duffel into the bed of his truck and I climbed into the cab. Streetlamps cast lonely cones of light.

Not too many people.

There's more in the summer. The truck kicked to life. So what did you think of the ferry?

Is it the same one that Charley took?

Sure is.

We swung out to a sinuous road. As we drove, he pointed out the school (no longer used), the post office (one employee), the Methodist church (summer services only). A line of squat brick buildings had been military housing; one still served as the police station. A state trooper came over every Tuesday. On Trooper Tuesdays everyone drove the speed limit.

In the fog the island seemed hunched and poor, white vinyl siding glowing eerily as we swept past, every house and tree haloed by our headlights. I too felt smudged and hazy, seeing everything through your eyes: the milkweed, bleached white by the car; the hand-painted mailboxes; the old Sunoco station; and the dark hills leading to the sea.

As we flew by a gatehouse, Johnny reached over and squeezed my knee. Then he yanked back his hand, and his cheeks flushed pink. In silence we surged past a cemetery. Then endless webbed fence.

Military.

Oh. Nice.

The road narrowed, and the trees grew close, short and squat with twisted branches. Dirt turnouts flashed in the high whites. The road grew gravelly, rough and broken.

Almost there.

I sensed this was something he always said right here, just as the touch of my knee was something he always did by the gatehouse. They were rituals of homecoming, full of the gentle unselfconscious assurances you give a sleepy lover. Something he might have said to you, for instance, that summer night when you had come, exhausted from the wedding, seasick from the ferry, back to his family home.

Time was a film, and I had inserted myself into your reel.

A rise. We were running out of land. When it seemed we would drive into the sea, Sykes House appeared: a blacker hole in the black sky. Massive. Like God had punched his fist through heaven. Johnny pulled into the driveway and chuckled.

Welcome to the castle.

~

THE HOUSE WAS COLD AND DARK and smelled of shut-up things. We stood in a dim kitchen the color of egg yolk, and I felt the cold settle in my stomach.

Johnny offered me a glass of water. You must be exhausted. He hoisted my duffel higher on his shoulder. Let me show you to your room.

Up a spiral stair we went, through an endless spill of bedrooms, to a big trapezoidal nursery with twin iron beds and a cot. Here, he said. You'll sleep here.

I had thought we might talk a bit, but after apologizing for the cold, and again offering me water, he kissed my cheek and left. For a long time I heard him creaking on stairs and clattering in the kitchen. Then the house swallowed him up.

It was cold in the room, very cold; I had not yet removed my coat or hat, and as soon as I was alone I shut the windows, but it made no difference: The wind whistled through the cracks, sighing.

A stiff stale sadness hung over the room, the thin bedspreads and faded carpet. Yet it was beautiful. The walls and ceiling were painted a dusky indigo, so that I felt wrapped in a bolt of denim. Tapered candles stood along the mantel; a gold fan was unfurled in the fireplace. On the wall there was an etching of a goose in profile, her long neck almost elegant. Everything spoke of care and deliberation.

Gingerly, still in my coat, I lowered myself onto one of the twin beds. The yellowed sheets smelled like crushed leaves. I pulled the wall lamp's chain. Darkness. The thin cotton quilt reached to my chin. I curled tight, creating a nest of body heat, sure I wouldn't sleep.

All night the wind knocked against the glass.

17

IN THE MORNING I WOKE TO WATER OUT THE WINdow. In the glassy square it glittered, the whitecaps rolling smoothly to shore. Last night I hadn't realized the beach was so close.

The wind had stopped; the morning was calm, and if it wasn't exactly warm in this blue nursery, at least the previous night's bone-chilling cold had eased. Drawing the quilt more tightly around me, I slipped from bed and opened the door. Nothing stirred in the dark wooden hall. Off the passageway I could see half a dozen doors, all closed.

I dressed quickly, hunched over my duffel, piling sweaters atop my sweatshirts, wearing nearly everything I had brought. In the warped vanity mirror I studied my lumpy reflection.

When I descended, I found Johnny on the back porch, wrapped in a leather topcoat, staring out at the sea.

Aha. She emerges.

Hello.

A little hitch of awkwardness. We had cast ourselves in the roles of host and houseguest, but it was too much. I stood taller. How long have you been awake?

Hours and hours. When I got up this morning, I looked in on you. You were sleeping like a baby. Breakfast?

~

THE KITCHEN WAS LONG AND LOW, with two farm tables end to end, and more dishes and glasses than I could count, dozens of mismatched mugs hanging from copper hooks and stacks of china plates in all sizes and designs. The stove was a witch's stove, black and magnificent, and the farmhouse sink had a copper faucet. Even in all my layers I felt small, maybe because here, like everywhere else in the house, the ceiling was painted the same color as the walls, so that I felt cocooned. This was a house that held you.

Coffee?

Yes please.

As he tapped the grounds and warmed the pot I studied the knuckles of his hands, dark with hair; the great trunk of his body, broad and sloping; the thick neck, half hidden by beard. There was something animal and hulking in him, which made his grace, when it came—there, as he cracked an egg high above the sizzling pan—more surprising.

Then it struck me that you had most likely sat at this very table and watched Johnny make eggs in exactly this way.

Did he feel it too, this doubling? When he had touched me in the car I was sure he was thinking of you, but now he gave no sign that there was anything uncanny about making breakfast for me in the way he had once cooked for you. Without ceremony he brought over our plates, thumped them down, and began to eat, quickly becoming absorbed in an old *New York Review of Books* open on the table.

I ate slowly, watching him. Waiting. Wanting some acknowledgment of my presence, of the strange and bold thing I had done, following him here to this cold and wind-blasted rock, to this crooked colorful mansion of antiques. We had never really been alone together; in New York we were always in public. We were both pretending, I thought: pretending this was ordinary. I coughed.

He looked up. There was egg in his beard.

It's pretty weird to be here.

You think so?

Isn't it weird for you?

He sipped his coffee. Not particularly.

The eggs were delicious, creamy, soft, buttery, with large curds and flecks of pepper. I edged some onto my toast.

So you've been, like, living here? Hanging out?

Pretty much.

Since that thing happened. Did it have to do with Gina?

He smiled, tight-lipped. You remember her name.

Even with the light on, even with gold paint, it was dark in this kitchen, and my toes in their sneakers were aching with the cold. Johnny's gaze wandered back to the newsprint.

So what happened?

What happened with what?

With Gina. I read her post.

He pushed aside the paper. Is that why you came here? To ask me that?

No.

I sounded like a child denying her hand was in the cookie jar. No, I continued. I came because you invited me. Remember? But of course I wondered about it.

Gina likes attention. That's all I'll say about it. That woman likes attention, and if she can't get one kind, she'll go for another.

A thousand questions buzzed in me, a hundred push-backs and interrogations, but I was suddenly conscious of eating his bread and sitting at his table; I was conscious, too, of the wrinkles in the paper from his tight grip.

Some women are like that, I allowed.

He continued to read; I wondered whether he was punishing me. Finally I said, in what I hoped was an entirely different tone of voice, You said you had something to show me?

~

A HOUSE BY THE SEA should be open, generous, proportional, with pine, glass, sun-dappled walls. It should invite the sea, but push it away, too, providing a broad vista when the sky is clear and ample shelter when it storms. Open and closed, light and dark, it must embody the flickering, liminal quality of the land on which it finds itself.

So said Johnny as we walked back through the house, before admitting: Sykes House did none of these things. Sykes had been a modest sea cottage until Johnny's great-great-grandfather had bought the neighboring house and built a kind of grand hall between them, thus beginning the meandering architectural adventure wherein each generation, larger and yet more determined to summer together, had added more rooms. So Sykes had grown, oozing its shingled mass over the rocky point, until Johnny's father's third wife had declared she hated the place and demanded they summer in the Hamptons instead. Since then, Johnny had pretty much been free to do with the house what he wanted, so he had thrown out "a lot of crap," repainted the rooms, and held on to what he loved.

As we toured, I tried to count: There were three spiral staircases, and close to a dozen bedrooms on each floor, all painted in the same saturated colors as my nursery room, walls and ceilings alike wrapped in a continuous silk of color. Goldenrod and topaz and pistachio, creamy terra-cotta, shocking grape. Rooms of hallucinatory color. And yet the house retained its family feel: These throbbing, glowing rooms were filled with twin beds, trundles, cots. Up on the third floor we passed a linen closet stocked with dozens of wool blankets and sets of sheets, embroidered pillowcases and old throws from New England prep schools, all neatly sorted and labeled. I could see summers past, guests rolling suitcases, sand in the floorboards, the singing of hot water through the old pipes. Big meals on the porch, swimsuits draped over the railings, childish feet pounding on creaking stairs. A home, with room for extra cousins and great-aunts, college roommates and new girlfriends. A home where everyone belonged.

He took me up some back stairs, and then down a short hallway with two doors, one of which, he explained, led up to his office in the tower. The other door, small and carved directly from the wall, gave me something of the feeling I had had as a small child, walking up to the Duchamp diorama in the Philadelphia Museum of Art. That door was made from battered boards and framed by bricks, and this was a modest white pine door, but somehow they had the same feeling of trespass.

A key unlocked it. Johnny ushered me through and shut the door behind him. My stomach knotted. That old ditty that you used to sing rang through my mind. *The queen is in the dungeon, the king won't let her out.*

Another flight of stairs, even tinier. Up here, the air was heavy, the ceiling low enough that Johnny had to duck as he led me along a narrow passage to the eaves. Here, in a big, low room that smelled like a Goodwill, there was a frilly

Victorian baby carriage and a stack of *National Geographics*, old end tables and a microscope, a rusted shovel, and a box labeled *Charley*.

Johnny stood among these objects, and though he was one of the most composed men I knew, a certain formality in his hands, the way his heels touched, told me he was nervous.

So, I heard about this trick.

Trick?

Thing. Technique.

He pried open the lid of the cardboard box. It was full of Ziploc bags, each one containing a single item of clothing. He withdrew one with a black T-shirt inside, its faded lettering reading FIORE DANCE. With that same curious formality, he unsealed the bag and stuck his whole face inside, breathing so deep his hair shook. When he raised his head, his pupils were dark.

God. He held out the bag. Go on.

The baby carriage probably belonged to someone long dead. The *National Geographics* were from 1912. No, I said.

Come on. He gave the bag a little shake.

The plastic stuck to my sweaty fingers. I sniffed. Very faint, but definite, yes: something like crushed crackers, and bergamot, and sand. You. Your smell. Your smell, in a bag, like you had walked into the room, like you had pulled me, squirming and giggling, onto your lap. I smelled the tacky peach lip balm you used to use, and the milky scent of your sleep. God, that black T-shirt. You brought it home after your first tour with Luciano and cut the neck out and wore it every morning, and now I could see you at the breakfast table, one knee up, with your mug of black tea, doing the crossword . . .

Not too much, Johnny snapped, and yanked the bag away.

What? Did—

No, no. He wiped his mouth. Sorry. I'm not used to sharing. You were fine. It's just, if the bag is open too long . . . and besides. That's an especially good one.

God, you're really sick. I laughed. You're really—I mean, this is creepy.

He laughed. After the annulment I was completely torn up. Wrecked. I wanted to hold on to her in any way I could. She stored a bunch of stuff here the summer after we got married, and when she didn't ask for it back . . . well, I wrapped it up.

I closed my eyes. You were almost in the room with us. A wisp, a hint, but so fragrant, so full of everything I had forgotten: that peachy lip balm, that shirt. The milky crushed-cracker smell of sleep.

We spent the rest of the morning in that cold round room, smelling you. A woolly hat, summer dresses, a bathing suit. Sweaters, an old hoodie, blue jeans. Some smelled like nothing, to be honest, though for Johnny's sake I pretended. Others, though. Others . . . there was a collection of your old leotards, all tangled together like mottled skins, and when I stuck in my nose, up came rosin, talcy deodorant, stale sweat, the musky smell of incense. It all came back. How I would sit on your carpet playing with your old pointe shoes while you burned stick after stick. How you carried your own rosin, not trusting what was in the box.

~

WHEN WE HAD GORGED OURSELVES, when we were dizzy and quiet, vaguely ashamed, we descended, and the ritual of the door was repeated. In the dove-gray parlor we lay down on the floor. I don't know why. Maybe, having done something so intimate, we needed to touch ground. All I can say is that when I saw Johnny on his back, with his shirt riding up, I curled beside him and set my head on his narrow white strip of belly.

Do you think she'll ever come back? I asked.

My head rose and fell, rose and fell with his breathing. He swallowed, a dry sticky sound. When he spoke, the back of my head vibrated.

I want to say something, but I'm afraid.

I stared up at the peeling paint on the ceiling, already cracked.

But sometimes, when we talk about Charley, I feel like I'm actually describing someone else. Like I'm not really talking about the person I used to know, but this mythic version of her.

Like we've been romanticizing her?

Yeah. I mean, she was actually quite troubled.

What?

She was troubled, Frances. Really troubled.

He lifted up his neck, and under my cheek his stomach muscles clenched. I don't want to disturb your image of her.

My head felt pumped full of air, like I had shot up thirty thousand feet in an airplane.

No. Tell me.

When I met her, she had a deep craving for discipline and structure. That's why she was so drawn to Luciano. He demanded absolute commitment from his dancers. He made a cult out of himself, and some part of her liked that. She liked having an outside authority to tell her who she was. Dance did that for a long time. Now I think the convent's filling that role.

He sat up on his elbows. My head rolled off his stomach, and I sat up too.

That summer on the island, being away from New York, and the company, she started to lose it. She was practicing all the time, like compulsively. Beautiful summer days, and she was locked inside. And then when she got injured, she didn't know what to do with herself. She had lost the structure of being a dancer. It makes a kind of sense to me that she would find something to take its place. Something even more extreme.

His eyes were shining. It breaks my heart. I really miss her. After she left, I could feel all the parts of myself dissolving, turning into nothing. And even now, when I think about her behind those stone walls, punishing herself, it hurts so much. It makes me want to go back in time. Which is why I do this dumb stuff. Keep her clothes in plastic bags. I'm sure you find it pathetic.

I don't.

His look was so imploring. I swam into his eyes. My skin tingled.

I hope she comes back, he said. I really do. But I don't know.

Me neither.

We were kneeling on the carpet, facing each other, and for a long moment it was holy. Then suddenly I felt scrunchy, almost gross, like when you stay inside too long on a sunny day.

I'm going to go for a walk, I said. I think I'll go back down to the ferry docks.

What? No. Let me drive you.

No, I need to walk. I need to get my bearings.

It's raining. It's actually a far walk. Let me drive you.

I stood. I'll walk.

Johnny wiped his hands on his pants. Fine. Let me get you a raincoat.

I followed him into the front hall where there were coats hanging from hooks. As he shuffled through them, looking—they were stuffed together, three or four deep, heavy topcoats and rain slickers and peacoats that smelled faintly of wet wool—I saw that the wall behind the coats was not solid but contained the outline of a door, cut from the wood paneling.

What's that?

Just a closet. He handed me a yellow raincoat, many sizes too large. I think this is the best we're going to do. You want a hat?

~

JOHNNY WAS RIGHT. Distances were deceptive here; even walking down the driveway took a long time. At the final curve, I looked back at the shingled house. From the tallest turret, a copper mermaid slowly spun, showing off mottled green breasts.

The road was long and black and winding. I walked with my hood down, fat spring drops splashing my face. There were no cars. There was nobody. I walked fast, and then slow, in the middle of the macadam, as if the trees growing tangled at the edge might twine their wet branches around me and pull me into the woods.

Finally I came to Mickey Mouse, painted on the road. A chunk of his head was missing. Then SpongeBob, and Snoopy and Elmo, masses of bright crumbly color. The night before, as we were driving to the house, Johnny had explained that kids painted the road each summer, and that people navigated by these cartoons, since there were no street names for the dirt roads that led down to the mansions. Quaint, I had thought, but now the teens' work seemed lurid: Here a Smurf was missing a chin, there a pink whale lacked an eye. They were sloppy, painted by teenagers nostalgic for a childhood they had barely left behind.

Below these thoughts was everything Johnny had told me, a big jumble of facts, like toys or weapons with sharp edges. I had to stay calm, I had to take each fact out carefully, the way he had taken out each item of your clothing. I shouldn't rush. This word, *troubled*. Like *troubled youth*, like *juvenile delinquent*, like a psychiatric report from 1942. Not a word I had ever associated with you. Well, I'd have to think about it. The thinking lay ahead of me like a long complicated project, but I couldn't break into it yet because I was thinking about the room. The locked room. Here was the thing: I was touched by that neglected low room, and those sealed plastic bags. They smelled, some of them, like nothing at all, they had become for him pure memory, and that touched me too; I had the feeling I was getting to know him, that he was letting me into the brick chamber of his heart, the private tower of his marriage grief.

The island was working on me. The island was not so much creepy as lonely, here in the damp neglected off-season, and it struck me that I had misjudged Johnny too as creepy, when really he was wounded.

The trees broke. A clearing of salt shrub tumbled to the sea, and then I was passing the low house where the cop stayed on Tuesdays, and here came a sidewalk, the vaguest sense of a town—church, post office—more solid in the daylight, and emptier too.

As I was wondering whether Johnny and I were completely alone here on the island, a truck came zooming along. There, in the window, a woman who looked remarkably like Tess from Café Lappet. Hanging out the passenger side, two shaggy white dogs. For the first time since arriving on the island, I smiled.

But surely it wasn't actually Tess? She didn't seem like an off-season island type. And Johnny would have mentioned her presence.

Unsettled, I walked on. At the ferry dock, I stood on the far edge of the pier and fished out my phone, meaning to call Mira, but then the thought of all her questions exhausted me. Later. I'd do it later.

The sound was filled with misty fog. Somewhere, the ghostly peal of a buoy. Beneath my feet, water slapping the pilings. Charley, I whispered. Charley.

18

WHEN I RETURNED FROM MY WALK, THE RICH DARK scent of roasting meat greeted me, and the dining room table had been set. In the kitchen, Johnny kissed my cheek, and I smelled sweat and garlic.

Ready to eat these ribs? What can I get you to drink?

I sat at one of the kitchen farm tables with an Aperol spritz and watched as he snapped asparagus spears. Idly, I told him I had seen a woman who looked like Tess driving a truck.

Could be. Her folks are still here.

She grew up here?

This rough, rainy place didn't fit at all with the woman I had met at Café Lappet, with her clingy fingers and big red mouth, the showy way she had touched him.

Sure. He chuckled. She's a townie.

There was something chalky in the way he said this, something thick and knowing. It was a private joke between them, this word, and it evoked everything: late summer nights, smuggled beers, bonfires. Necking on the beach. I drew my nail along the table's seam, right where the oak had splintered.

So you've known her a long time.

He was turning a leek beneath the faucet, pulling back its fronds.

In a way.

He started in on another leek, washing and chopping. The pale green circles fell like coins.

We were both on the island as kids, but we only really got to know each other about six years ago.

Right after Charley—

Yes.

The sweet plummy smell of roasting meat twisted in the hot steamy air.

He kept talking then, about being a summer kid, the long afternoons and nights, swimming, fishing, learning to drive his father's boat. He spoke too of the local kids who knew every cove and held the summer kids in casual contempt, the sons and daughters of handymen and landscapers who ran in their own groups and had their own rites. He told me how much the summer kids longed to be accepted by the townies, the particular shame of being rich and soft, and how everyone knew Tess with the purple hair, Tess who had the best singing voice, Tess who quoted Sylvia Plath and gave boys—Johnny clarified he had never believed this but still, it was said—blow jobs in the bathroom of the commuter ferry.

By then we were both sitting at the table with glasses of melted ice and he had been talking steadily for half an hour, maybe more, but I never interrupted him, not once; I sensed he was unlocking another door to himself.

Tess was such a saint, listening to me go on and on. I really was hung up on your sister. I didn't realize she had fallen in love with me until it was too late. God, that was awful, getting out of that. But she was a real champ about it.

And now you're friends.

My past just—he waved his glass around—piles up around me. It accumulates in these relationships. I can't let go of it. I've never been able to let go of people. Or things.

I flicked my eyes to the attic.

Exactly. I'm not sure why I'm telling you all this. Something in the way you listen gets me talking. He looked around the kitchen. Well. These ribs need to cook. I'll do the vegetables later. Want to see the studio?

What studio?

I built Charley a studio.

I followed Johnny out the back door and across the lawn. Beyond the grass there was the sea. Ahead of me he walked, tall and straight, with his hands curled loosely into fists. He had said that he could never let go of his past, but I could see now that it was much more than that. He clung to it. He built monuments to it.

The studio, though, was not a monument, only a low building of pine sheltered from the sea.

I let out a whistle. You built this for her?

He closed his eyes, and then unlocked the door.

They say that dance studios are the same the world over. They say that no matter where a dancer goes, or how far she travels, once she walks into a studio, she is home. The marley floor, the wooden barre. The mirrors that cover the wall. Here was no exception. The studio was small, but the floor was sprung, and frosted glass admitted weak island light.

Slowly I walked in a circle. When I stopped, Johnny was watching me.

We stood facing each other. There was blue in the air. In a dance studio, before the lights come on, there is always blue. It comes from the blue-gray marley, and the blue-white walls, and the mirrors that scatter the light from the sky. I've always liked it, this blue. It takes me beyond the discipline and repetition, beyond the pain and shaking, to that space on the other side. Ballet's dreaming ease. Something like that dreaming ease opened between us, and into that ease Johnny said, I hear you've been going to Luciano's classes.

Who told you that?

Paul.

I stared. Paul Sonette? The dancer?

He stepped toward me, so close that I thought he was going to touch my hair. You know I know Paul, he said softly. You don't have to do this innocent girl routine. It doesn't suit you.

I stepped back. I wasn't under the impression that you spoke regularly, I said stiffly. He didn't tell me that.

Johnny laughed and pivoted away, swiveling his hips. What did you learn in Luciano's class? How to move from the inside? How to listen to your body?

Something soft and mocking slithered in his questions. But he looked so ridiculous circling his hips that I had to laugh.

Come on, Frances. You don't like my dancing? Show me what you learned.

Now the rhythm in his hips was traveling to his ribs, and then his shoulders, through his neck and arms. Never would I have thought that Johnny Fitcher would let himself look so goofy. I softened my knees and swiveled my hips, floating my arms and rolling my head, and Johnny did the same. There we lolled, teasing, testing. Dancing. He swung into an arabesque like a dog playing fetch: big and floppy, his leg flailing out behind him and his head flying back.

Laughing, I circled him, floating in that loose improvisatory way that Luciano had invented and that my sister had loved. Johnny fiddled with his phone, and bass filled the room, nervy and pulsing, something cool and yet hot, insistent: It boiled in my blood, familiar but new, slippery.

What is this? I shouted, and he shrugged, pretending he hadn't heard me. So I turned my back to him and danced, listening to his feet squeaking. Suddenly he was very close, brushing my back. His chest was broad and warm, and as I leaned back, he swept his arms around me and fit his chin against my shoulder, his ear touching mine. From his chest came a rich low rumble, a cat's purr, as if he were teaching me new sound, new language.

Beautiful, he said, stretching out the long vowels. Beauutiful.

Weak in the knees, I turned and kissed him.

His lips were plush, his stubble scratchy. He smelled like the kitchen, and he kissed me like he was ready to eat.

We kept on, and there was something exploratory and friendly in it, two animals saying hello. We made a thorough inspection of each other's face, and then his hands began running along my sides hungrily, the way he had touched me the previous night in the car, as if I had fur running the wrong direction and he needed to smooth it down.

Frances. He cupped my face. It felt very nice to have his big flat warm hands around my cheeks. Is this okay?

This is okay.

As we kissed, his hands lifted my shirt. With a twist he unhooked my bra. I sucked on his fat lips, shivering without my clothes, his massive hands warming my skin. Peeled like an onion, I felt raw, sparky, and free. Off came my jeans. Ineffectually I tugged at his shirt. He scooped me up, wrapped my legs around his waist, and backed me into the doorway. I dug my spine into the wood and my feet into the jamb. His fingers gently pushed me open.

When he carried me back to the wall, my eyes locked on my reflection: the pointed toes and clutching arms, the big eyes. To see what he saw was intoxicating. I looked and looked. Then I whispered, I feel like a monkey, dropping my weight onto his hips.

You weigh nothing, nothing, I could do this forever, he said, and tenderly poured me onto the floor. Too quick, he slipped inside. Digging, scraping me out, he wrapped me in his arms so tightly I couldn't breathe, and that was when I felt him go to another place. From him, this high feminine cry.

Afterward, we stumbled across the lawn with our arms around each other, staggering. Johnny might have been singing.

19

BY THE TIME THE RIBS WERE READY, THE RAIN HAD started again. The drops plunked the windows and drummed the roof. I sat at the transformed dining table, sipping a glass of Burgundy. The wine pricked my tongue, light and peppery. Like a stretch of silk, I felt taut and soft, expensive.

At first I had found the dining room silly. The rosy walls and foamy-green mantel clashed the way candy stings your teeth. But when I saw the room at night, I understood. Lit by dozens of candles, the pink mellowed, and the gilt mirror over the fireplace multiplied the flames, so that I felt cradled in the heart of a glowing music box.

Johnny emerged with bone china bowls. The ribs were nestled on a bed of creamy polenta, cradled by spears of asparagus, brilliantly green and blistered. Wow, I said. Wow, wow.

I don't know how the ribs came out. The sauce didn't reduce as much as I thought it would.

It looks amazing.

I took one bite of everything right away: polenta like a tangy cloud; asparagus grassy, smoky, plump; leeks like spring; and ribs like winter. Oh, the ribs. Easily they slid from the bone and lay like velvet in my mouth. Lavishly I praised it all. Beneath his dark beard his skin flushed pink. His big paws moved awkwardly over the table.

It's fine, he said. The ribs are a little tough.

The pork bloomed in my mouth. No, they're perfect.

He blushed again. It was interesting. Before today, he had resembled an impassive sculpture, his pale face hidden by a thatch of dark curls, and the ice-chip eyes, looking beyond me to the realm of ideas, until they didn't, until they suddenly fixed on me, demanding something extraordinary. But half an hour had changed him. He was open to me. When I spoke, he turned the color of a split seashell; he turned the color of the walls.

At first we ate in silence, relishing the fat, the cream, the flavor. Then we began to talk, but the lazy, languorous chat of people who have been to bed together. Rain dashed the window glass.

I took another sip of wine and felt the air loosen.

So, I said. When did you know?

Know what?

With my head I indicated the air between us.

The furthest thing from my mind.

No way. You never thought about it before this weekend?

He leaned back, drained his glass, and poured himself the remainder of the bottle. Sounds like you did.

How to say that I had known for a long time without ever looking directly at it?

In the museum. That first time. You touched me. You were thinking about it then.

I touched you?

You put your chin on my shoulder.

Saying it brought back the cool quiver of his curled ear. He had done it again in the studio.

I was probably feeling very affectionate toward you.

You really don't remember? I was telling the story about going to the museum with my dad, that room that scared me—

Oh yes. His face lit up. *Étant donnés.*

What?

Étant donnés. The Duchamp that frightened you. You're right, that was a sexy story.

My face flushed as I remembered how I had stumbled over the words, trying to describe the splayed headless woman.

You know. He ticked his glass, and the wine sloshed, purple-red blood. I played a little trick on you that day. I actually know *Étant donnés* quite well. It's an important work of art to me.

But you let me describe it.

He rubbed my thumb with his nail. As I said. It was sexy listening to you.

Between my legs something soft, gold, and heavy. I saw then how sex was something that amused Johnny. A plaything that gave him pleasure to adroitly maneuver. I saw this, even as it worked on me, even as I was maneuvered.

The thing is, he said, Duchamp would have loved your reaction. That feeling of shame, that self-consciousness as you look through the peephole—that's not an accident. It's intrinsic to the artwork. It's intrinsic to all art, actually. Especially Western art, which, let's be real, is basically a whole lot of gawking at female nudes. Male gaze, all that. But by making his female nude visible to only one person at a time, by forcing each viewer to peer through a peephole, Duchamp is making us confront the inherently voyeuristic nature of the entire Western artistic tradition.

As Johnny talked, he pushed back from the table and unfurled his hands, ease and expansion radiating from him.

The story about how it got made is wild. Duchamp was one of the most famous living artists when he announced that he was giving up art for chess. For the last twenty years of his life, everyone thought he had stopped. But he was working away, in secret, on *Étant donnés*. He told very few people. It wasn't discovered until after he died. He called it an homage to erotic love. He worked on it closely with his lover, whom he used as the model.

If he loved her, he should have included her head.

Johnny laughed. After their affair ended, Duchamp got involved with another woman, and then he began to incorporate her body into the diorama, too. So it's a model of many women's bodies. It's sort of a Frankenstein woman.

I studied him closely. You know a lot about this.

He shrugged. As I said. It's important to me.

Wrongness had suffused me when I walked up to that door. Right away, I recognized that the architecture belonged to a nightmare. Children know these things. The dark room had swallowed me. Legs and arms tingling, I had approached the holes of light, expecting to be grabbed from behind, sucked through the door, stabbed. Something.

There was a man, I said.

A man?

Yeah, this man came into the room. He was laughing at me. Laughing at the little girl looking at the dirty picture.

Maybe it was your superego.

What do you mean?

That sense of shame that we were talking about. Being a voyeur. Maybe you were anxious about being caught looking, and so you hallucinated the thing you feared. Being watched.

Maybe. I thought about it. Why do I feel so ashamed when I look?

Johnny shrugged. Beats me. I love looking at naked women. I don't feel bad about it at all.

~

UNTIL THAT NIGHT I did not know the sea could hold so many colors, that from inky black could swirl indigo and emerald, pearl and silver. Wrapped in the fur coat of Johnny's dead grandmother, I sat in the prow of his boat, looking back at the streaming bubbles of custard cream.

It was cold and dark and clear after the rain. The stars overhead pricked painfully. In the middle of the bay, Johnny cut the engine, and the boat lurched. Far off, I could see the gray shapes of summer houses. Johnny plunged his arm into the bay and pulled up a cube of mesh. Covered in oysters, it came dripping into the boat. He wriggled his eyebrows.

You're not full, are you?

With a long shucking knife Johnny freed a shell before dropping the mesh back into the sea. Tucking my chin into the bristly fur, I watched Johnny drive in the knife, forcing open the shell. He smirked as he offered me the misshapen body on its bed of blush. I slurped the sea. I sucked a body. I was eating a creature that had been alive a moment ago. A creature that might still be alive as it slid down my throat.

We feasted that night. Intelligently his knife flicked over the animals. Another, and another, and—another. The depths glimmered.

Doesn't the farmer mind?

My father owns the farm.

In the bottom of the boat, salt water sloshed over our shoes. As Johnny sank the last oysters, I thought how those pearly shells would be shipped on ice to the city, where, in a loud restaurant with smoked mirrors and shimmering bottles, a man would order them for his date. I could see it: her gold hoops and bare arms, his tailored shirt, the pearly oysters in their rough shells. The cold brine. His laughter, her teeth. Johnny. I realized I was picturing Johnny. Johnny with another woman. Wet and salty. Everything else glinting glass.

20

I WOKE LATE THE NEXT MORNING, MY HEAD HEAVY from wine. All night, wind had gushed through the windows like water, and I was stiff and aching from the cold. But also happy. Under the covers my body found a cozy nest of warmth. I lingered in it, remembering.

His whole body had come wriggling and frantic against mine, so that sex felt like being sucked under by a wave. It was not a hot point of touching, not the sweet searing of nerves. No, with Johnny it happened everywhere on my body, and it happened to him too.

Off to the nursery with you, he had said afterward, stroking my hair affectionately, and I didn't think to question it. I was wondering what we were going to tell people when we got off the island; I was imagining my mother's surprise and hoping that his father liked me. Far off was the thought that someday I might be very rich.

For I knew he was with me now. When he had stroked my thigh, in the car back from the ferry, I was sure he had been thinking of you, and even in the dance studio, down on the floor, I hadn't been sure he wasn't burrowing back through his memories. But last night, in the boat and in his bed, I had been me. Frances, he had said. Frances.

The hall was dark and still. I walked through a bedroom with pea-green walls to another hall. At his door I tapped my fingers. Darkness within. I tapped again, more loudly, and stepped inside. The bed was made, the coverlet smooth. A white dress shirt lay discarded over a chair.

For a crazy moment I thought he had left. Then from below I heard the thump of the refrigerator door, and boots on tile. Some whistling. I smiled. He was already making breakfast for me.

~

WHEN I WAS THIRTEEN, I went to the city to visit my father.

Deliberately Johnny buttered his toast. He buttered slowly, pausing to let the spread soften before smoothing it. His comfort with waiting for his pleasure to heighten interested me. Finally he took a big bite of toast and brushed the back of his hand across his lips.

Even on the train I didn't think it would really happen. I thought my dad would cancel at the last minute. But there he was in Grand Central, right by the clock, waiting for me.

The clock, I repeated. Johnny had never told me anything about his father before.

He took me over to his office and trotted me out in front of all his employees. They made a big fuss over me, of course—the boss's son. I remember this one guy gave me a cigar. They were all grinning and shaking my hand. Everything was so gray inside that office—gray carpet, gray walls, gray paneling on the cubicles—but out the window I could see Central Park, this perfect rectangle of bright green.

Afterward he took me to one of those ridiculous Midtown steak houses where they still think it's 1985: white tablecloths, waiters in suits, the whole thing. At the end of lunch, with great ceremony, he brought out this black jewelry box. Open it, he said.

Butter sheened Johnny's lips. Open it, I told myself. Open it.

Inside was a Rolex Day-Date. Do you know what that is?

Such a look of expectation on his face! Not really, I admitted.

They call it the President. I think four or five of them have worn it.

Carefully Johnny sliced his egg in half. I tucked my leg under my butt and picked up my fork, but I didn't eat. On my plate, my fried eggs sat like twin yellow suns sealed in skin.

Finally I asked, What happened?

Nothing. After lunch we went to the bank and he put the watch back in our safety deposit box. He told me when I was twenty-one, it would be mine. The whole afternoon had been pure theater.

I reached across the table and pulled up his sleeve. So where is it?

Johnny finished chewing. He took a long, deliberate swallow of coffee.

My father didn't want me to major in visual art. He was dead set against it, but I insisted. I was eighteen, he couldn't stop me. But I think he hoped, right until the very end, that I would join the family business. I had been groomed for it. Obviously. Even when I was running around with purple hair, doing the experimental theater lab at Bard, he still thought I would grow out of it. But after college I moved to Brooklyn and joined a squat. After a while he stopped asking. He started preparing my brother instead.

And the watch? Did he give that to your brother too?

No. It was mine, he had given it to me, there was nothing he could do. He didn't even find out I had sold it to pay for photo equipment until months later.

Johnny gave a nasty laugh, smug and childish. I thought of our father, smoking his pipe, speaking from the side of his mouth. The hard, bitter thing in Johnny's laugh came into my chest.

At least he chose you. At least you were the chosen one.

Johnny's eyes narrowed.

I could never get my parents interested in me.

Your name hung in the air between us. Your name always hung between us, but now it was a knife I was holding out before me.

He coughed. Tell me more.

When I was little, I used to hear the way my parents talked about Charley's dancing, and think that I couldn't wait to grow up and be worthy of my parents' attention in the same way. But by the time I was fifteen, it was clear that I was nothing like Charley. I didn't have her talent. She was always going to be the better version of me.

How illicit, how wonderful, to voice these petty thoughts! Maybe this hard, bitter thing had been in me all along, and Johnny was helping me find it.

My father was never really into me either. This was more like some last-ditch effort to get me to shape up, but I think he had his eye on my brother the whole time.

Really?

He shrugged. Really.

God, what is it? Why does God make you fall in love with things you don't have the talent to do? Why does he break your heart in this way?

Oh, but I like the way you dance.

Shut up.

No, I do, I really do. Even yesterday in the studio. He blushed, there was something so endearing in his blush. It's not like Charley's, it's got a more interior feeling.

I made a face.

No, I mean it, Frances. You're very sensitive. You've got this rich interior life, and it shows up in the way you move. I see that. Honestly, I've often thought you should get back into dance. You gave up too soon.

My knee's trash.

Okay, maybe not ballet, but modern. Not—for I had wrinkled my nose—not with Luciano, nothing like that, something else. I could see you going in a postmodern direction. More conceptual. Subtle. You've got nuance, Frances, that's the thing. You pick up stuff in the world and you translate it onto your body in this beautiful way, and honestly, fuck those directors who couldn't see that when you were young.

I didn't look at him. My eggs shimmered on my plate.

Listen, you've been in Charley's shadow your whole life. That's the truth of it. And Charley, I mean she was an amazing technical dancer, and she had that bravado, but she didn't have this acute sensitivity, this responsiveness. I think you should get back in the studio. He nodded solemnly. You've got to get back in there again.

I'm so out of shape.

Take the summer. Audition in the fall.

He laughed and pulled me to my feet.

Look at you. You want to. It's all over your face.

But—

Oh, you're so cute when you worry. Come here.

Where—

Here. Right here.

~

POOR BOOPSIE. Tenderly he drifted his fingers along my inner thigh. Poor good Boopsie.

I lay on the floor with my head against his belly, as we had done yesterday. Back then, the move had felt risky, thrilling. Now his squishy belly noises comforted me. Boopsie? I asked.

What, you don't like the name? You seem like a Boopsie to me.

Into the square of sunlight falling on my face I grimaced. The heat was intoxicating, stupefying. I closed my eyes.

Sometime later I asked, But what about you?

What about me?

What about your art? We were talking about your dad trying to get you to go into business, but you don't care about business, you're an artist too.

Ha.

He sat up; my head flopped off his torso, and I sat up too.

I haven't done that in a long time.

I thought you said you were into video these days.

As soon as I said it, I realized the double meaning. Now it was Gina's name that hung in the air between us.

But if he was thinking of her he didn't show it. Shrugging, he said, Nah, not really. I fuck around, but real art, that's hard.

But if you love it—

Nah. Not that much. He put his hands on his knees. His shaggy chest hair was shot through with gray. Come on. What do you want to do today? Want to go to the beach?

~

IT WAS A FUNNY THING about beaches. (Really it was a funny thing about money.) Though I had spent four years in California, it was the miserable stone beaches of New England that enchanted me. They spoke of restraint and hardship, vigor and discomfort, values that Puritans and ballerinas share. A tropical beach seemed gauche. Give me the freezing Atlantic.

All of which is to say, as soon as I saw Henrietta Beach, I loved it. Off a rocky dirt road, down a steep spill of steps, it was gray and narrow, windswept and chilly. The sand scraped pleasantly underfoot, and the ocean stretched out, gunmetal gray with flecks of green.

We spread our towels on the sand and smeared sunblock on each other's back. If we were together, this was how it would be. A ridiculous thought. But I had it, and I marveled, not for the first time, at how I had hidden this reality from myself during the long winter, how I had known and not known it.

I felt close to you. I know that sounds strange. But everything—the bumpy drive over gravel roads, the cooler of sandwiches, the brush that grew on the dunes—you had seen and done. We shared it; we shared even Johnny standing, holding out his hand, saying, C'mon.

At the water's edge, beer-colored surf purled around our ankles.

Let's go in.

Are you serious? It's freezing. And I can't. I tugged at my jeans.

He raised his eyebrows. There's no one here.

In my underpants I felt delightfully free. The sun warmed my back and shoulders as I laughed and danced back down to the sea, my hands by my belly.

Aww. He pouted. I thought you were going to skinny-dip.

I punched his shoulder. I will if you will.

Back at our towels, we stood thumbing the elastic of our underwear. Over his shoulder I could see the scrub brush swaying, and a single gull. Something prehistoric in this, something that made me imagine we were the first humans here, alone on this island with only birds swooping over the salt grasses, the steady lonely thwap of the ocean's waves.

Go, Johnny said.

We shucked our underwear and ran screaming to the sea, his dick flopping, my breasts swinging painfully, his belly like a bear's, dark and furred. The water whomped the air from my chest and I fell into it, yelling without sound.

For as long as we could, we flailed and ducked under waves and came up shouting. Then we ran huffing back to the blanket. As I was wrapping my towel around me, I glanced up at the cliff. There, on a rock beside Johnny's truck, was a lone figure watching us.

I touched Johnny's arm.

What? He was toweling his back.

There's a—

But when I looked again, they were gone.

Shivering, we stretched out and let the sun do its work. Salt pricked my lips, sand coated my elbows. We pointed out animals in the clouds, dozed and read our books. Sometime later we ate the roast beef sandwiches Johnny had packed. Johnny drank two beers and got up to dance, swirling his hips, laughing at my embarrassment, saying, Come on, show me something.

So I taught him a simple phrase, laughing at how he jumped and spun around, at his clumsy lumbering and earnest questions, and as I moved, I was aware of new pleasure in my dancing, a certain pride and snap in my limbs. He had called my dancing beautiful. Subtle. I unfolded my hand.

Was that it? Johnny leapt into the air and spun around. I burst out laughing. No, come on! he wailed. Give me a break. Show me again. I'm going to get it, I am.

In the city he held himself so gingerly upright, as if his body were a container of water threatening to spill, but now, here, on the island, he flopped, he lunged into jetés like a Labrador, he was unafraid of looking ridiculous, and for a moment it made me love him.

When we were fully exhausted, we flung ourselves down on our towels and he cracked another beer. Balancing it on his belly, he said, There's one thing I've been wondering this whole time.

Guilt like a fever flushed me. I don't think Charley would—

What? No. Oh my God, no.

We eyed each other. It actually makes me, I started to say, just as he said, All that was so— And then we stopped.

No, he said in a stronger voice. All I was going to say is, You really don't have a boyfriend? Have you ever had a boyfriend? You're such a mystery to me.

I laughed, flattered. There's been some people.

Who? When? He flipped over to his stomach and propped his head in his hands, a girlish gossip. Your fans want to know.

I hesitated. There was a boy in high school. And last year, there was this guy, well, he had a girlfriend, but we would mess around sometimes.

He scoffed. Men are monsters.

The tattooed bike messenger with the sad wolfhound eyes glimmered before me, his smell of cereal and sweat, his apologetic air.

He was nice, I said. I mean, he was a cheating asshole, of course, but he was nice to me. I didn't find out about the girlfriend until later.

Do you still talk to him?

Sometimes. He's not a bad guy.

Johnny raised his eyebrows, then flipped onto his back, playing a game with himself where he tried to keep his beer can level on his belly. I felt I had upset him somehow, though I couldn't see why. We talked about his ex-girlfriends all the time.

The sun got higher in the sky. Some kids arrived, and their voices floated down the beach. Johnny wedged his can in the sand, draped his shirt over his eyes, and began to snore.

I was restless. Antsy. Careful not to wake him, I rolled off my towel, slipped on my damp jeans, and headed to the rocks.

Down at the cove's edge, the water pooled at the bottom of the boulders, green black and brackish. I hopped from stone to stone. White scaly remains of mussels feathered their undersides. Down below I imagined subterranean things, crabs with pinchers, little fish trapped by the outgoing tide. The pulpy kelp clung to the rock.

When I looked back, I saw I had gone a long distance from our towels. Johnny resembled something dead and forgotten, sleeping there on the beach. I regretted telling him about the boy. I didn't care about him. Here on the island he was far away. Everything was. Mira. I should text Mira.

When I finally made my way back, Johnny was sitting upright, his arms wrapped around his knees. He didn't turn his head as I sat down.

You were gone a long time.

I was exploring the rocks.

He looked over. His face was flushed with booze and sun, his eyes tiny and red. He looked like a dangerous animal, stunned and surly.

I didn't know where you were.

In silence we packed our things and folded up the blanket. The whole ride home, the sun was in our eyes. Johnny shook out a pair of sunglasses from the center console for himself, but I was left to squint, my hand in the air.

21

FROM THE BEDROOM I COULD SEE HIM ON THE patio, a glass of something dark in his hand, staring down the blackening blue sea.

~

AGAIN IN THE LURID PINK dining room we ate his meat. For the hundredth time I wondered why he had painted the ceiling too, why he had wanted every room to swaddle and squeeze his guests. Trying to be convivial, I asked him how he had chosen the colors, and whether the ceilings had been difficult to do, but the answers he gave were vague and monosyllabic.

When our plates were empty, he turned to me with a curious, sickly grin.

I lied to you today.

You did?

My father didn't give me the watch. He gave it to my brother.

Oh. I was confused. You didn't go to the city—

That was my brother. He's younger, by the way. And he loves the watch, and he wears it every holiday, right there on his wrist where I can see it.

Oh.

He shook his head. I was such a disappointment to my father. I didn't play sports, I didn't make friends, I had this funny walk. I liked role-playing games. I mean, I get it. *I* wouldn't have handed the family business over to me. But some part of me has never been able to accept that instead of running a $4 billion real estate company, I'm like, serving on the boards of small downtown theaters. Or I *was*. And occasionally fucking around in the studio to keep myself amused. It's pathetic.

I thought you didn't make art anymore.

He lifted his head. Fine. I'm even more pathetic.

That's not what I—

No, Frances, I'm a loser. Charley knew it. She saw that in me, my deep inherent stupidity. That's why she left me.

Pain like ragged lines sizzled off him.

She left you because she found religion, I said quietly. Right? But she loved you.

God, I don't even know, he said sulkily.

No, you do know. She found religion. Right? Or am I missing something?

Charley Charley Charley! he exploded. That's all you care about! Look, I don't know why she's in that fucking convent, I don't know why she's so crazy, or if I made her crazy, or whatever, and frankly, Frances, it hurts my feelings when you pump me for information like that. Can't we drop it? Once and for all, can't we drop the question of what happened to Charley?

I wasn't—

Well, that's what it feels like! Every time her name comes up, you pounce. Fuck, you even hallucinated that she was watching us on the beach today. You're never going to let us get out from underneath her shadow.

It's not like that—

Do you even care about me at all?

Johnny, I do.

As I spoke, a kind of gallantry gathered in my chest, an intoxicating, ennobling feeling.

I do, a lot. I really care about you. Which is why it hurts me so much to hear you talk like this. I'm sure you didn't drive her into the nunnery, I didn't mean to imply that. You don't need to worry about Charley. She loved you. And you don't need to worry about your father. I mean honestly, fuck your father. Fuck that company. They just, what, gentrify neighborhoods and fuck over poor people? You don't need them.

He glared. You don't know anything about it.

And now that ennobling feeling widened, it turned into a basket that could hold all his pain, and I couldn't resist the thought that he would be so grateful to me, he would love me the way he had loved you, if I could only get him to open up.

Tell me.

No. There are some things I can't explain.

Okay. But the point is, you've built a life of art and beauty, and I have to believe that has more value than anything your brother's doing. Or anything your father thinks.

Ha.

You help the avant-garde thrive! You bring new art into the world! That is the significant thing. That is what people will remember a hundred years from now.

I looked at him at the end of the table, with his big black beard and his hunted blue eyes. How many times had he told his brother's story of the watch from his own point of view? When had he invented those details about the cigar, and the park laid out in its fluffy green rectangle? Looking at him, I saw the boy he had been, or thought he had been, awkward and dorky, a perennial disappointment, and I wanted to tell him that I would accept him, exactly as he was.

Softly I said, It's awful that your father did that.

When I stood to hug him, I saw over his shoulder the dark shape of the door.

~

THE SEA WAS a sound in the dark.

Behind me Johnny pulled me close and kissed my neck. I can't talk like this to anyone else, he whispered.

I spun in his arms. Tell me anything.

My heart in my chest swelled like a basket, growing. It could contain anything.

Look. He pointed. Jellyfish.

In the next wave I could see them, a swirl of transparent tentacles borne up by the heavy swell, glowing white in the midnight blue.

I trembled, and he pulled me toward him. He was beautiful in the moonlight, big and hulking, his eyes dark pools in the shadows. All those nights in the city rose around me, candlelit dinners, the hungry way he had looked at me. It was not about you anymore. It had stopped being about you a long time ago. There on the lawn with the dark sea licking the shore, I finally understood that.

Then he was pushing me down. I resisted. Laughing, he tugged harder, his thumbs under my breasts, until I was down on my knees and he was inside me. It hurt, it was too fast. But it was intimate, too, it was like his confession, abrupt.

Afterward in his arms I felt coddled, comforted. Stay, he whispered.

Stay?

Stay. I don't want you to go. Stay here with me.

Johnny, I've got class tomorrow, I've got . . .

Boopsie. I won't let you go.

22

DEAR CHARLEY,

As you probably guessed from the postmark on this envelope, a lot has happened to me this spring.

What I have to say is difficult. In January, Johnny came back to New York. When I heard the news, my first thought was of you. I began to think about the past, about what, exactly, had happened in your marriage. So I reached out to him. I wanted to see if I could get him to talk.

We ended up spending a lot of time together, and now I'm here on Cup. I'm writing this from the back porch, looking out at the bay, as you must have done. I don't know what to say, Charley. We were never that close, not really. But I feel close to you now.

Love,
Framces

~

DID YOU NOTICE that when I signed my name, I put an extra hump in the letter *n*? Framces. It looked like I didn't know who I was. I decided to leave it. What did it matter? Either way you would sense my ambivalence.

I wanted to tell you everything in that first letter, but only a few sentences came out. I told myself it didn't matter, that you would understand the important parts. I trusted you to get what I was trying to say.

~

SLIPPING FROM MY NEW YORK LIFE was surprisingly easy. The Franklins responded to my text about extending my vacation with a thumbs-up emoji. Mira flooded my phone with worried questions, but in the end she had nothing beyond reminding me I had a term paper due. With our folks I simply didn't mention where I was; once when I was talking to them on the docks, pretending I was in New York, the ferry's horn blasted, and Mom cried, That ambulance sounds very strange!

The ease with which I left my life convinced me it had never been my real life. The moment I agreed to stay, a little gripping thing in my head relaxed, as if I had taken off a hat that had never fit.

~

ONE AFTERNOON AS I SAT on the porch reading, Johnny banged through the screen door with a big cardboard box.

Open it, he puffed.

Inside were smaller boxes, and inside those boxes, nestled in tissue paper, was the kind of clothing I had seen on other women in New York but never known where to buy or how to afford.

Two linen dresses, in sand and black, a cashmere sweater of pistachio green. For the beach, a white cover-up—I suppose my ragged hoodie hadn't escaped notice. But best of all, a quilted jacket in shard-like blues and greens. I shook it out from the box and shrugged it round my shoulders.

It looks good on you.

I pulled at the material. Dozens of colors shimmered in the weave. The jacket was a big warm cocoon, nipped at the waist and cuffs, which gave me—I saw in the window's reflection—a jaunty, insouciant look. I had never thought of myself this way; it was Johnny's choice, Johnny's vision of me, and yet it felt exactly right, exactly who I wanted to be. Even if I hadn't known it.

Johnny was watching me, a little half smile on his lips. Open the other one.

Here I found ballet slippers, tights, leg warmers, knitwear, and two leotards, one pale pink and the other mint green.

What's all this?

I'm not saying you have to go dance. I just want you to have the option.

I ran my hand over the clothing. The leotards were my size; he had even chosen the brand I liked. How did he know? Well. It was the brand every dancer liked, and I was not his first dancer.

I've got clothes in New York, you know. I could've gotten them.

I had meant to tease, but Johnny turned pale, then flushed pink, as if I had pressed hard on his skin before letting go.

I want you to be comfortable.

I hugged him then. Throwing my arms around his neck, I whispered, I am. I really am.

~

EVERY MORNING NOW, I gave myself barre, and I made it hard. Hundreds of tendus, balances and adagios I repeated until my legs were trembling and my new leotards stained with sweat. Like discovering I could still sing, this dancing; like discovering all this song still stored within me. I had carried it this past year, heavy like a stone. What a relief to transform it into music.

As I moved, the clothes in the attic kept coming back to me. I realized that until the box of sweaters and leotards had arrived, some part of me had been afraid Johnny would make me put on your clothes. That he would say, in his offhand way, The weather's getting warmer, feel free to take anything of Charley's you want.

But that had not happened. He had bought me my own clothes. He had seen my own particular style; at dinner that night he had said, *She had bravado, but she didn't have that thing you have. You've got nuance.*

Slowly his words, which had been hovering somewhere above my skin, sank down into my skeleton. Slowly I moved all the way through you to something else.

I began making little exercises for myself. Messing around. That's what I called it, messing around. In every little exercise I gave myself I tried to channel not you, but the yearning you lit in me.

It hurt to be opening again. After I had tried so hard to move on, to make another life, it hurt. But right away, there was also nowhere I'd rather have been. So I put *that* in my movement too. I danced, holding in my mind the candle of this question: Why did dance have such a hold on me? Why couldn't I be free of this dream of ease?

There, alone in that blue room with the mirror stretching from corner to corner, I confronted myself. I looked at my body, still the same old body. But I could see what it wanted now. Using the mirrors, I studied how it used space. Not like yours; it didn't devour the air. It coddled it. Nursed it. Split it. Could I make the gesture more precise? Slow it down? Could I end the diagonal on the left leg? No. Maybe. Again.

Three or four days, this time I'm describing, but it felt longer. Every night at dinner Johnny told me how much he believed in me, saying I was sensitive, beautifully aware, and every night in bed he manipulated that sensitivity until my body buzzed.

Was he making me or uncovering something already deep inside me? That buzzing, I tried to translate onto my body. This feeling: Something monstrous is crawling from me.

This one time—but I might have been imagining it. This one time, I was lying on my back with my eyes closed, drawing big half circles to loosen my hip, when suddenly the air darkened. A figure at the window. Even without opening my eyes I could feel it. Johnny.

More slowly now I circled my limbs, imagining him watching me, thinking that I had gone through the dungeon door of my childhood, I had broken into the diorama that had so frightened me, the forbidden room at the back of the museum. He was the man with his eye to the chink in the door, and I was the headless woman lying in the dead grass with her legs spread. From my hand, an illuminating lamp.

~

THEN JOHNNY HIT ME DURING SEX. It made the room twist. A sheen slicked the darkness. I didn't like or dislike it, the slap was not connected to pleasure, not yet. It bent us to a new shape.

Later in the mirror I couldn't stop looking at myself. The red splotch on my ass transfixed me. Every morning it was the first thing I checked; every evening I examined it anxiously. The red darkened to mottled purple and blue.

He did other things to me, things I can't bear to tell you. Always it was the same. A cool prickly astonishment, and then my body buzzing.

Gradually I understood: He had unlocked a door at the back of the room called sex. In this back room there were the usual things, orgasms and moans, but striated by violence. I saw, not without regret, that now that he had unlocked the door beyond the door, that first way of having sex was lost to me forever. I would never be content with mere tenderness again.

In your studio, I danced close to the mirror, eyeballing myself. Was it visible, what he had done, on my face? The darkness of becoming his creature wriggled out through my hands. Fluttering.

~

TWO MORE THINGS ABOUT THIS TIME: I had no idea what he did all day, shut up in the dark house, alone with his thoughts and papers. I didn't ask, and he never said. Yet I felt connected to him, as if by a fine metallic wire. Done with dancing, I would look up at the house, black against the blue sky.

The second thing is that while we still talked about you, the way we did it changed. We still talked about you as a dancer, and I spoke about our childhood, all the dancing we had done together, but we never again mentioned your marriage. Skillfully we steered around that black ice.

~

WE MIGHT HAVE CONTINUED ON like this indefinitely, but as the weeks passed, Johnny's mood soured. He had decided the porch needed to be power scrubbed for summer, and that he would do it himself, but there seemed to be a great deal of drama about who had a power washer and when he could pick it up; I gathered it was connected, however obscurely, to old feuds and feelings about his father, but he never explained anything, just muttered and mumbled, until one night in bed he growled in my ear, I hate this island sometimes! Let's take a trip.

I giggled. Okay, where?

He rocked me back and forth. France.

No.

I was terribly frightened.

No, not Paris, not France, I don't want to go there.

The walls of your abbey would be shut to us, and I could not bear to make that journey only to be turned away. Nor could I stand to be in Paris with him. It would make me think too much of your first trip with him, back before you were married, when you were first falling in love. No. He had to take me someplace new.

He chuckled, a little gurgle at the back of his throat. Okay, my little Boopsie, then where?

At the time, the night winds still came whistling through the cracks in the casements, and even with my blue jacket of sky I was cold at night. I named the first warm city that came to mind.

Rome, I said. Take me to Rome.

23

YOU LIKED NEW THINGS, DIDN'T YOU? I DON'T mean that as a judgment. But you liked to buy things, and you never had trouble spending money. I mean you liked it when people spent money on you, it didn't make you uncomfortable. You didn't see why you shouldn't have nice things, especially if someone else could afford it.

Do you remember when you stole from Mom? You were fifteen, and you desperately wanted a new leotard. Mom said you had plenty of perfectly good ones, and it wasn't her fault if you had cut them up and pinned their backs. You two fought about it, and then one morning before school you must have helped yourself to some twenties from Mom's wallet, for that night you had a horrible row that culminated in Mom demanding that you bring your dance bag to her.

When Mom found that black leo with the purple trim, it was not a moment of triumph. She held up the black cotton thing, and for the first time I saw how wrinkled her hands had become, how her blue veins now bulged. Her jaw locked.

Go. Get away from me.

Later I heard Mom and Dad arguing about it. Dad wanted to know why the hell you shouldn't have a new leotard, and Mom, after mutterings too low for me to hear, abruptly wailed, The Visa bill is *totally* out of control!

I hated you then. I hated you for costing them so much; for the first time in my life I judged you. You were selfish, and self-absorbed. I was eight years old, I didn't exactly know those words, but I felt clearly that if you had known the pain you were causing our parents, you wouldn't have done what you did.

When you became a star—that word is clumsy, but you really were—and I realized I never would be, I thought this hardness must be part of the reason. You took what you needed. All my childhood I knew exactly how much ballet lessons cost; for years afterward I kept hearing *The Visa bill is totally out of control!* I felt responsible for that bill, for every bill I created. Even now, though I loved Johnny's gifts and wore the sweater and jacket every day, I also couldn't stop thinking about their cost. They implicated me in an agreement I didn't fully understand.

But you wouldn't have worried. Not the old you. You would have said, If we're going to Rome, I need something to wear. You would have sent Johnny links with sizes and colors marked; you would have breezily said that he could afford it. But me, I asked about the thrift store.

On my walks around the island I had noticed a clapboard sign hanging beneath the church's mailbox. *Consignment Shop. Open Wednesdays 10 a.m.–2 p.m.* Oh yes, it's real, Johnny had said when I asked. You should go. It's unbelievable what the women on this island toss.

It smelled like dead people's clothes down there, mothballs and sloughed-off cells, bitter cleaner and BO. The white-haired woman sorting jackets frowned at me, as if she were trying to recollect something, before curling back her thin lips in a smile.

Every time I left the safety of Sykes, I felt conspicuously on display. I love the solitude here, Johnny said, I love the quiet. But it didn't feel quiet to me. Out on the road, walking to town, or down at the beach, my back to the cliffs, and certainly here, with the woman looking at me, I felt the island's eyes, I heard their questions, I wondered if they looked at me and remembered you. I could never decide how much we looked alike.

Now I shuffled the hangers noisily, flipping back necks to read tags: Ralph Lauren, Marimekko, Anne Klein, great fistfuls of designers. A felt flag with a white dove and a lopsided rainbow hung crookedly on the cinder-block wall above a clutch of brocaded sweater sets. LOVE, the flag said.

The woman coughed; a bell chimed.

Barbara, I've got the girls outside, do you mind?

Before I remembered her name, I knew the voice. Red lips, black hair. I turned to study a puce Patagonia fleece.

Frances! Frances, is that you? Tess cried.

She gushed over the coincidence of finding me here, she wanted to know how long I'd been on the island, she pinged me with a dozen fast questions, did I like it and what did I think of Sykes and so intense, right?

The colors. She shivered theatrically. The colors, right? I told him, it'll make the place feel closed in, but that's the way Johnny is. If he likes something, he's got to do it all the way. Paint the walls *and* ceiling, right?

As she talked she kept two fingers on my wrist. When I drew back my hand, she grabbed it again. Her heavy makeup, eyeliner and mascara, blush and bloody-red lips, made her face a fleshy, mobile mask.

So what brings you to our little shop? Johnny probably raved about all the cast-off treasures, didn't he? Here, let's see. There is unbelievable shit in this place, I mean it's unreal what people on this island give away.

She winked and went back to flipping through the hangers. Now, let's see, what will suit you?

Oh, you don't have to—

My dogs are outside. Abby and Zoe. Have you met them yet? I'll introduce you when we're done here. Here, try this on.

She thrust something pink at me.

Oh, I can't—

He's taking you on a trip, isn't he? And you don't know what to wear, and you're in a panic.

I could only nod. Of course. She was the best friend, she had seen women like me come and go. She knew so well the pattern I fit inside.

You've got such a cute body, you dancers have such incredible legs, you're so fucking *lithe*, *lithe* is the word, isn't it?

She seized my arm and squeezed as if testing for doneness, then stuffed the pink dress into my hands. Really. Try it on.

I looked around uneasily. She laughed. There's no dressing room! Over your clothes.

I put my tote bag on the dirty linoleum floor and lifted Johnny's pistachio sweater over my head before folding it into a soft green square. Behind me, Tess's breathing came in shallow, eager huffs. I pulled the sundress over my head and pushed it down over my T-shirt and jeans.

Yes, she cooed. Adorable! You've got to get it. She flicked the price tag in my armpit. Forty-five? Well, I'll talk to Barbara, she'll knock it down. Oh my God, Frances, what do you think?

She pushed me before a full-length mirror. The dress, pink gingham, ruched at the bust, was for an insipid Bo Peep.

Get it, she hissed in my ear. I know what Johnny likes.

Quick as a ferret she dove her hand into the flat bony concavity between my breasts. And it'll give you some cleavage, and *that* never hurt anything, now did it?

I can't.

Her bony, red-tipped hands reached for me, but I spun free.

I can't. Thank you, but—

Oh, you dancers are so afraid of showing some skin! They raise you like nuns, don't they? But Johnny likes his ladies feminine. He'd never admit it, but it's true. That was the problem with me, I wasn't femme enough—

Frantically I pulled at the dress, but the nipped waist got stuck around my ribs. The word *nuns* strobed my brain.

I can't, I can't, I'm sorry—

As I yanked up the dress a stitch popped, and up came my T-shirt too, exposing my belly. Then I had the thing off, and I was pushing it, all crumpled and torn, back into her hands and making my escape.

I saw you.

At the steps I stopped.

I saw you that afternoon at the beach with Johnny.

I pulled my tote higher on my shoulder.

You don't like me, Tess said, and I don't blame you. But I'm going to tell you this. Being with Johnny changes you. Before I met him, I thought I wanted to be a writer. But I was really terrible. And he helped me see that. I mean he helped me see that my real talent is editing. He helped me get my first job in publishing, too. He changed my life. So don't think I don't know what you're going through.

Maybe I nodded, maybe I simply fled. Outside, two big white dogs gamboled in the grass, sniffing. The smaller one stayed back, studying me with alert eyes, but the larger one came forward, her big tail swaying, and pressed into my hand her cold pink nose.

~

WHEN I GOT HOME, Johnny was sitting in the doorway shucking corn. I heard you ran into Tess.

Oh, did she text you right away? I pushed past him. Your little spy.

Boops! he called over his shoulder. You can't let her get to you. She was teasing you, okay? She's sniffing you out.

Ha.

Oh, you're cute. Look at you, you're adorable when you're mad. Now come here.

I've got to go change.

Oh come on, Boops. Come *here*.

24

IN ROME THE ANGELS WERE BIG-MUSCLED BOYS with swords and thick thighs. I walked along in the cruel bright sunshine licking gelato di crema and staring up at their inscrutable faces. Johnny bought a tomato big as my face, dark red and glistening inside, chambered like a heart. With milky fresh mozzarella we ate slabs of it, and curls of prosciutto thin and translucent, and pale green melon balls; we lived in a world of peach and gold and white weathered stone. We gorged ourselves on frescoes and cherubs, Berninis and Caravaggios; there wasn't a church we didn't enter or a candle we didn't light. Soft-bellied Madonnas with cool impassive faces, nymphs twisted in gorgeous terror.

We stayed on the top floor of a narrow building, behind a green door with a gold flap for letters. In the heat of the day we made love in a square white bed beneath the airy duvet, deep in the darkened chill of the apartment with the cornflower sky blazing outside, red roof tiles gleaming in the afternoon sun. Later in Campo de' Fiori we watched a vendor throw bursting red fruit at a man, screaming; we laughed at the Italian-ness of it, the cliché literalized.

We were close in Rome, staying shoulder to shoulder as we navigated the hot streets and dark churches, interlacing fingers at café tables, sleeping every night like two commas floating in the white sea of down. On Cup we still slept apart; he had said that he slept better alone, but he hadn't rented two apartments, and so every night we snuggled together, and he woke refreshed, he even began to say he was sleeping well, he liked having me close.

Sometimes as we sat on a bench or walked by the Tiber, Johnny leaned against me, not pushing, not erotic, but relaxed, companionable. I liked that. And I liked that he needed me. For all Johnny's sophistication he seemed ill at ease in Italy, startling at the foreign tongue, and so it fell to me to page through the phrase book, to order our espressos and ask directions. The sense that we needed to rely on each other bound us together. For the first time I felt what it might be like to operate as a team.

Sure, he paid for everything, as he always did, but it was nothing too lavish. Our apartment was only a studio, and we picnicked there more than once; we went to modest trattorias and stayed far from the luxury shops, which relieved me. I wasn't his pet but his equal.

One evening as we watched the stray cats pick among the ruins, Johnny said, Being here makes me think about how after everything is gone, the only thing that remains is art.

And roads.

What do you mean?

I shrugged. There's Roman roads everywhere. Right? Old cow paths in England, turns out the Romans made them.

Sulkily he traced a numeral in the granite. But you know what I mean. Like this. Someone, a real person, made this mark, I mean carved this exact stone two thousand years ago. It makes me feel so small.

His frown disconcerted me. Really? I said. You don't feel connected to the man who made it? Like, part of some beautiful unfolding chain through time?

No. His voice was dead. No, it makes me feel like a big fat nothing. Like if I can't make something decent I'll disappear forever and none of it will matter, nothing at all.

His mood hadn't blackened in Italy before, and I wondered whether there was something I had done. Carefully I pressed my hand against his.

We had a good evening, sitting on a terrace forking up fried artichokes and spiny black things from the sea. Ambling back along the curved streets, we competed to name the colors of the buildings: Champagne, he said, biscuit, blush, dawn. Cream, I suggested, salmon, apricot, rose, and he laughed, and I really didn't give his melancholy another thought until I awoke, in the blue light of dawn, to Johnny smacking himself in the face.

Babe, I gasped.

Rhythmically his palm bludgeoned his nose.

Babe, babe. What are you doing?

I'm a loser, I'm a fucking loser. (Smack.) How can you stand to be with such a loser? How can you even (smack) stand it?

In the filtered yellow streetlight he was demonic, his skin chalky and stretched over his skull, harrowed, one of Michelangelo's damned.

Johnny, stop. Stop it.

How can you even stand to be with such a fucking loser? Your sister couldn't stand it, how do you put up with it? My art is shit, it's complete rich boy shit.

Your art is not shit.

It's complete garbage. That's why I had to give it up. It's— He slammed his fists into his forehead. It's shit.

Johnny! I seized both his hands and brought them trembling back down to his lap. Looking him deep in the eyes, I murmured, You're not, that's your father's voice in you, but you're not, you're really not, and while I sang that song to him, the feeling that I was a net, spreading myself beneath him, came back to me. I can hold you, I can hold anything inside you.

Slowly his breathing quieted, his fingers uncurled. I suck, he said softly. I suck hard.

You don't suck. Making art's hard. But it's about the process, right? It's about doing it. Everything else is ego.

He looked at me. His eyes were red and small and uneven.

Maybe you're feeling bad because you haven't done it in a while. Maybe if you get back in the studio, you'll feel better.

He snapped free from my hand.

I don't know who you are.

Electricity coming off his body.

I don't know who you are, that you could be with such a shit artist as me.

I didn't answer, and when we woke, a few hours later, to proper morning, bright yellow and hot, we didn't speak of it again. As usual we strolled to the corner café that was already beginning to feel like our regular spot and spoke about the day. He wanted to go back to the Villa Borghese, and though I had no desire to look at more art with him, something in the way he pulled off puffs of croissant made me disinclined to argue.

It was more complicated than it should have been, getting there. We couldn't find a taxi, I didn't want to walk; somehow we ended up on a packed bus where the threat of pickpockets made me clutch my purse to my chest, and between that, and rerouting due to a strike, and my inability to speak Italian, we missed our stop, a fact that I observed calmly as the bus pulled away.

What? His face distorted with purple rage.

I think we should have gotten off there.

Then why didn't we? he roared. What the fuck is wrong with you?

What's wrong with you? I snapped. At least I was paying attention.

You're such an idiot, he hissed. A woman with a baby clucked her tongue at us.

Later I cried; I kept saying it was unfair, how angry he had been. He seemed genuinely baffled. You messed up, he kept saying. You messed up, and we missed our stop; of course I was going to be upset. It's only natural.

I thought, but did not say, that he had missed our stop too; I thought, but did not say, that he was punishing me for the night before, for witnessing him in his self-loathing. And: Hadn't he done the same to Charley, long ago? But I was too scared to mention this.

In my house that's always how it was, he mumbled.

What do you mean?

That's how it was. If you messed up, even if it wasn't your fault, you got yelled at. I can remember my dad, like, losing his shit on vacations when we'd get lost.

Did you like that?

No, not particularly.

Well then.

~

ON OUR LAST DAY in Rome he bought me a pair of crimson stilettos, along with wine and cave-aged cheeses in waxy white paper. When he presented the pink shoebox he hung his head shyly, like a schoolboy.

Try them on.

That this was a kind of apology I understood, but I didn't like it. He had yelled, he had been terribly unfair, and I wanted to hear him say it; I had been cool to him, these last twenty-four hours, waiting for the words I was sure he owed me.

Try them on, he repeated.

The heels were blood-red satin, with elaborate straps that would bite into my calves once I had lashed them up. I could picture it—and then I was picturing you, laughing at the Tulip as you thunked down your whiskey glass. Locked in an enchantment I couldn't break. I had been so young, so childish, and maybe I was being childish now, putting so much stock in talking, clinging to some need for him to spell out his regret.

It's love, love, love, you had sung. *It's stupid loooove.*

I stepped into the sculpted beds, I fastened the little gold buckles. When I straightened, he sucked in his breath. Turning me to the dressing mirror, he stripped off my summer frock.

I watched the girl in the mirror as he kissed her neck. I watched as he unclipped her bra and took her breast in his mouth. His long fingers slipped over her belly, down into her, and she went slack-jawed with pleasure. Then he was tipping her forward, and she relevéd; then he was pushing into her and I fell against the mirror, braced myself, saw myself.

Look at me, I wanted to say. Look at me. But of course he already was.

25

IT TAKES A TRIP TO MAKE A HOME. YOU WERE THE one who told me this, back when you first started touring, but I didn't understand what you meant until I moved into an apartment of my own, a crappy bungalow in West Hollywood that I shared with three other dancers. By then you were gone, vanished behind the stone walls of the abbey, so I couldn't tell you how that apartment, which had seemed so cheap and strange, embraced me the first time I came back from visiting the East Coast, how my Degas print and old teapot comforted me, and even the furniture was dear. I couldn't tell you you were right: One had to leave and then return to fully claim a place. Now, the irony that you had vowed never to leave the abbey did not escape me. How could you know the convent was your home if you never left it?

All this came back to me when we were rolling our suitcases onto the ferry. In the back of the car from JFK I had slept heavily, slumped against Johnny, my brain fuzzy with jet lag, but once on board I felt wide awake, jostled by the summer crowd. The sun, gold and dying, reminded me of my first ferry ride, when I had flung myself across this same dark bay, feeling the wind snap and the waves slap.

It's so gorgeous, I exclaimed now.

Mmm. Johnny was tipped back against the bench, his eyes closed. You get used to it.

Affectionately I patted his knee. Poor guy was tired. From over her phone, one of the matrons stared. Blatantly I eyeballed her back, keeping my hand on his knee until she looked away.

On the serpentine road that marked the island's spine I thought about the girl I had been four weeks ago, riding in this same blue truck, with this same grizzled man. So timid, so naive. Now everything between us was easy and familiar. When we passed the gatehouse, Johnny gave my thigh a squeeze, as he had done before, murmuring his *Almost there*, but this time his hand lingered, and he didn't blush.

~

I WAS GLAD TO HAVE HAD his warm hand on my leg, that flush of his affection, once we got to the house and without ceremony he dropped his bag, grabbed the mail, and disappeared up to his office. Over his face had come that impassive blankness that suggested my presence annoyed him, and I stroked the place on my leg where he had touched me, thinking of it as a token guaranteeing my readmittance to his affection.

Somehow it surprised me to find Sykes as we had left it. The same heavy, dark furniture, the same rooms of splotched, saturated color. Yolky yellow, purple grape, grassy green: Each bedroom leapt to life when I flicked on a light. I turned on many lights that night. Walking from room to room, I looked at everything, though I wasn't really seeing the model ships and copper samovar, the leather-bound books and heavy wool blankets; I was remembering the girl who had first seen them. How scared she had been. All this had been foreign to her, and she had been so cold, wrapped in blankets or a shapeless heap of layers. Now the house held the day's warmth, and I walked through Johnny's rooms as if suspended by an invisible string, ballet proud.

He was unlocking me. But maybe I could unlock him too. For I simply didn't believe the cruelty he had shown me in Rome. I rejected it. Inheritance from his father. Behind some rusted-shut door he kept his goodness. The solidity of his hugs, the goofiness of his dancing, the sweetness in his fingers: Those were real, those were the hints of who he could be.

~

WE ATE A SIMPLE DINNER that night, too tired to talk much, though as Johnny cleared his plate, he said, I've got to go back to the city tomorrow.

Really? Why?

He had his back to me. There's a board meeting. And some business I should take care of.

I joined him at the sink, dropping in my plate and saying, with the same falsely nonchalant tone, I'll come along. I really should be getting back.

Back to New York? Why?

All at once I felt annoyed. Did he not know that I had another life waiting for me? There were my parents (who kept saying I seemed distant and threatening to visit), my classes (school was long over, but I could have summer classes, for all he knew), my friends (Mira kept texting, asking when I was coming back). When we had swung through New

York before our flight so I could pick up my passport—the black SUV idling on Clinton Street, me taking the stairs two at a time—one of the Franklins had stared at me as if I were a ghost. Where have you been? they said. Where on earth have you been? And I stuttered out an answer and spun out of there, blue book in hand, before they could ask more, but I could feel them studying me. Yes, he acted as if I had come to him wiped clean of any history, but it wasn't true. I had a life. Brusquely I turned—and saw on his face such a look of pleading.

Boops, I'll be back by nightfall. Do you really need to get back that badly?

I should.

In the sink he put his plate over mine and drew his arms around me. Holding me close, he whispered, But you're dancing again here.

I can dance in the city.

Yeah, if you rent studio space, or take a class. But here you've got privacy. You've got all the time you need. You really want to give that up?

I hesitated. He drew a finger along my arm.

You know, I spied on you in the studio one day. I peeked in the window. You're really getting somewhere, Frances. The way you move: It's you. It's not a performance anymore.

Stop. You're flattering me.

He held me by the shoulders. I'm not. I'm asking you to stay. Okay? Stay the summer. Finish what you've started.

Laughing, I pushed him away. Let's start with tomorrow. Summer we'll talk about later.

Good, good. He reached into his pocket and drew out a ring of keys. I'll only be gone a day. And I don't think you've made a proper study of the house yet. There's a lot of art, a lot of actually quite valuable art, in the rooms I keep locked up. Have a look around.

Okay. I reached out my hand, thinking to humor him.

He dangled the keys higher, out of reach. There's one thing. You can explore all the rooms, I don't care. Go back up to the attic, try on Charley's things. Whatever.

But what?

He pulled from the ring a small, oil-stained key.

Stay out of my office. It's nothing, just that room at the top of the tower, but I'd rather keep it private.

Of course. I would never.

He slipped the key back onto the ring. Otherwise, go anywhere you want. I'll be back by nightfall.

I'll miss you.

He bit his lip, his forehead notched. Sure.

No, really. I will.

He kissed me then. Hard, with a slick of teeth.

26

ALONE IN THE NURSERY, I THREW MY DIRTY clothes into the hamper and unwrapped the crimson heels. Nestled in their tissue bed of carnation pink, they glinted as if dipped in blood. I held one to the dim nursery light, wondering what exactly I had promised by accepting them.

~

THE NEXT MORNING, I knew right away he was gone. The silence was the kind of silence that follows a disaster, hushed but charged, as if the long halls and twisting staircases had collapsed around me. Stretching beneath the covers, I pointed my toes. Maybe I too would softly implode without him. Already I feared all the hours ahead.

The keys. Then I remembered the keys. They were sitting there on the dresser, by an old lantern. Still in my nightie I crossed the room and picked them up. Oil had left the smallest one smeary with iridescence. So small, that little key, only as wide as my forefinger, with sharp teeth.

I did barre that morning, alone in the studio, shaking off the pasta dinners and wine from Rome, but my body was stiff and uncooperative. After grand battements I lay on the floor in my knits and studied the ceiling. By telling me explicitly not to use the key, wasn't Johnny giving me permission? If he truly hadn't wanted me to use it, wouldn't he have taken it with him?

No. If this was a test, I would pass; I would respect his privacy. I made myself get off the floor and do some flat backs in the center, but my dancing was slack now that he was gone. A dancer doesn't exist without an audience.

So, scooping up my water bottle, I summited the hill. A warm June morning, and the bay was bright blue and lapping the shore, the dogwood in bloom. Beautiful. But my hands were stiff and cold. In the kitchen I depressed the French press too fast and hot coffee sputtered everywhere, scalding me.

After scrubbing down the counter and floor, I went to the dining room and sat at the long white table. A crust of dried jus from some dinner long ago splotched the paint, and I picked at it with my fingernail. The room was dark, the curtains drawn against the midmorning sun, the pink so toothy it hurt. The ceiling the same throbbing salmon as the walls. The dried wax from our melted candles had hardened into great grotesque glops, and I picked at them, too, and then dug at the white slivers under my fingernails.

I was lost. Embarrassing, but true. When I had asked to go with him yesterday, it hadn't been because I actually wanted to return to my ordinary life. I didn't want to be alone.

What to do, what to do. I couldn't bear to leave the property and risk running into Tess, or even one of the matrons with their dyed hair helmets. (Without him I had no courage to stare them down.) I couldn't dance. I wouldn't go into his office. But—the thought came to me sinuous, curled—perhaps I could poke around. Surely that would be okay? Yes. After all, he had invited me. He had practically insisted on it.

~

THERE WAS SOMETHING monotonous about Sykes, I decided that morning. The haphazard way each generation had slapped another wing or boxy balcony onto the shingled Queen Anne gave it an oozy incoherent feeling that quickly became repetitive. As I wandered through the second and third floors, I kept opening doors and finding not rooms but entire new halls; yet these halls had the same shut-up bedrooms as the other wings. Back when the Fitcher clan had been big and close-knit, the house must have been so happy and full—once again I could almost hear the sound of slamming doors and running showers and feel the sand gritting the floorboards—but now it was still, stuffed with fussy antiques and dusty treasures, glassware and candlesticks and etchings of sour aristocrats in pearls and lace.

I did have to unlock each room. The rooms in the hidden halls were kept locked. But if there was valuable art, I did not see it. Finally I sat on the top step of one of the staircases, the keys dangling from my hand, disappointed. There really was nothing. Should I go back to the attic and take another look at your bagged clothes? Probably, but it smelled even more musty up there. And those sealed bags made me feel like you were dead.

Then I remembered. The door under the stairs.

As I made my way back to the kitchen and front hall, I was reminded of going to the bike messenger's dorm. Every time, I would tell myself to turn around, that I was doing a bad thing. (I had known about the girlfriend, I had lied to Johnny about that.) But once I started, once I reached his hallway with the scuff marks on the baseboard and pale room numbers, I had to keep going, I had to knock. Even now I could see his black bike shoes outside his door, the spare wheel, his cap. Ordinary things lit by a spectral, sexual glow.

Some of that same glow now suffused the yolky dull kitchen and brightened the front hall. As I took down the rain slickers and Patagonia shells, the quilted plaid and heavy corduroy jackets, I told myself to stop. But the latch was lifting, the door was swinging back. In the dull yellow light, wooden stairs. Not a closet, but the basement.

It took me a long time to get down those groaning stairs, into the tang of roots and damp. Slowly I descended, sure that I would find something horrible. Bodies, blood, knives. But at the bottom of the stairs, there was only a workbench scattered with nails and a bunch of family camping supplies: sleeping bags hanging from hooks, big open tubs filled with flashlights and mildewy tents, a dinged-up kayak with life jackets piled inside.

On impulse I ran my phone's light over the workbench, and found, amid the screwdrivers and handsaws, a slab of wood, no bigger than a pincushion, stuck with perhaps two hundred nails.

I picked it up. The nails had been slammed at all angles, colliding with the wood grain, jutting from the side, twisted and bent.

How kind, how kind he had been to me all these days, and yet in the morning hours when I had been in the studio he had come down here and punched the nails. I knew it. The noise absorbed by cement walls. The bang of hammer. Doing nothing, nothing but wasting time; nothing, nothing but giving shape to his rage. *I punched a wall.*

Still sometimes I think that if I had not found that strange spiky object, I wouldn't have violated his trust. Before the basement I wanted to believe he was as he represented himself. But that spiky crucified pine heart terrified me. Not for a minute did I think it was old, or the warped project of his father or a friend. I knew it was his.

Upstairs, I rehung the jackets on their hooks. Then I fingered in my pocket the ring of keys. There it was: the smallest one with its serrated teeth.

~

IN OUR HOUSE there was a thing about privacy, wasn't there? I can remember Mom saying to me that big girls needed their privacy, that when your door was closed I couldn't simply open it, I should knock and wait and listen for your answer, a ridiculously elaborate and formal ceremony (it seemed to me) for a person who was always glad to see me, and who was nothing less than a god to me. How could you have anything to hide?

Soon that very word, *privacy*, with its beautiful soft pop in the beginning and the undulating hills of its final syllables, came to be synonymous with the blank varnished white of your shut bedroom door and all that lay beyond, with the strange smells of eau de toilette and powder deodorant, and the sight of those gauzy pink curtains you hung over Mom's sturdy cotton ones, so that finally the word *privacy* itself suggested to me layers of drapes that could, that should, be pulled back.

Rifling through Johnny's desk was a trespass of boundaries that even twenty-four hours ago I would have declared beneath me. After all, the reason Mom cared so much about privacy was not that it was disrespectful to go where you had not been invited, but that it was tawdry and common. It was a lapse of taste. And with Johnny especially, I was aware of taste.

But as I climbed the stairs, heading for the hallway that led to the tower, I didn't care about taste, or respectability; I didn't want to be a good girl. And when I had found the narrow door at the top of the spiral stair, when I had fit the little oil-stained key into the Yale lock and the tumblers with a sigh had rolled over, when I was standing at last in a pale blue room with a massive desk and ergonomic chair, I didn't feel regret or hesitation. I was owed.

First I tried the computer, but it was locked, and neither *Charley* nor *Sykes* was the password. Six drawers were built into the desk. I started with the top left one. Inside, faded receipts and USB drives, a pair of cheap sunglasses, paper clips and highlighters, an old birthday card from his mother. *Happy birthday, my darling.* Why did Johnny never talk about her, why was it always his father?

Methodically I opened all the other drawers. His checkbook. A money pouch with leftover euros. His passport. Though we had just traveled together I hadn't yet seen it, and for a while I studied the waxy face with its awkward, secretive grin. JOHN PRYCE FITCHER. Well, I hadn't known his middle name was Pryce. That was something.

There were hanging folders of tax returns and health insurance EOBs, some leases and bank statements, and if I had been interested in Johnny's finances or health or real estate, I could have made a careful study of them, and probably learned some outrageous secrets, but it all looked tedious, I didn't think it led anywhere near his heart, so I didn't bother. Somehow it disappointed me to discover that the great aesthete could have anything as ordinary as a junk drawer or tax return. Where was his secret self, the one that withdrew to watch me from behind a smile, or raged from that chalky Michelangelo mask of the damned? Where was the letter, the document, the object that would give me his innermost core?

I began flipping through the mail that had arrived while we were away. Bills, credit card offers, fundraising letters from the Hodge and New York City Ballet. The usual stuff. And then: a stiff square envelope stamped PAR AVION.

That spidery script. I recognized it right away. As if your teenage cursive had been poured through a palsied hand. (What are they doing to you, there in the convent?) I would have recognized it anywhere.

The envelope had been slit, and through the serrated tear I edged out a single thin sheet. *Dear Frances*, it began.

I blinked. Returned to the envelope. How had I missed the address? *Frances Garbinski, c/o Johnny Fitcher, 10 Elderberry Lane.*

Dear Frances,

As you can imagine, your letter caused me great distress. It is very bad that you are on Cup Island. Thinking of you seeking Johnny out, meeting him for dinner, getting sucked into his New York life displeases me, but the fact that you are on the island is very bad.

Please don't think I write this out of jealousy or judgment. In all the years of prayer, I have given the grief of my marriage over to God. No, I write today with concern. Get on the ferry. Leave today.

Love,
Anne

At first, all I could think was that you had written me back. I clenched the note. You had replied. Nothing else mattered. I smoothed the page against the blotter, looking at the cursive. There you were.

Then your words soaked me, as if I were a napkin darkening as I absorbed a spill. *Very bad. Leave today.*

I tried to shrug it off. Wasn't *Stay away from Johnny, Johnny is dangerous* all anyone had ever said to me? My father, Paul Sonette, Mira. *Stay away.* This was nothing different. This was you being you, indulging your dramatic streak. Exaggerating.

I dropped your letter back onto the pile of mail, only I must have really thrown it, for somehow I upset the entire pile and had to spend several minutes gathering up all the catalogs and bills, wondering hopelessly whether it had been in any kind of order.

Finally I sat back on my heels. There were dust bunnies by the radiator. A skin of dirt on the rollers of his chair. Last night at dinner he had known about your letter. He had seen the envelope, addressed to me, and opened it. Then he hadn't said a word about it. He had kissed my face and kept it from me.

On the shelves, among the folders and files, there was an old laptop, turned on its side as if it were a book. I took it down, assuming it would require a password like the desktop, but to my surprise right away you filled the screen, beaming at the lip of the stage, in a copy of the photo that had run in the paper the day after your debut, alongside the review calling you a major new talent, a significant star, and though the critic's words hadn't been written at the moment the photograph was taken, his anointment was there in your dark eyes, the wide-open way you basked in the audience's applause. You knew it, and it touched me that Johnny had chosen this photograph for his background. I remembered what Paul Sonette had said: *He doesn't mind when a woman is more successful than he is. In fact he likes it.*

Then I noticed at the bottom of the screen a folder named WOMEN.

I clicked. Of course I clicked.

Inside, a stack of files. Some of the names I knew, some I did not. *Gina*, the newest one was called. *Fatima*, *Analuisa*, *Kim*. *Theresa*, *Krista*, *Charlotte*, *Mims*.

I started with *Kim*. I didn't know Kim, had never heard mention of a Kim, thought it would be safe. The file date: six months after you took your novice vows. Who was Kim? A fireplug flat on her back, chin down while Johnny pumped above her. The camera caught her floppy breasts and spread thighs, dimpled in fluorescent light.

I slammed the computer shut. Gross. Oh it pleased me to call it gross, it gave me a sickly pleasure. Monster, monster. Remembering Gina's post. *Against my will, he kept videos of me* . . . Yes, that was what he had done, that was what men did, take and take. I cracked the laptop again and opened all the files, one by one, at first scanning, thinking it was diligent to confirm the content of each video, not to assume. More sex, harshly lit, flat. Did the women know they were being filmed? They never glanced at the camera.

But soon my cursor slowed; I let each video play for thirty seconds, a minute, two, riveted by watching him fuck. Some things he did, he did with me, and others were new: a slap on the face, not hard but deft, with the back of his hand. One woman he tied to a chair. Another he forced to her knees. Tears glinted in her eyes, her throat convulsed. That was the roughest stuff. The rest was tame. Just sex, in all the usual positions, with all the usual sounds. I was fascinated, and then bored, and then fascinated again. The little way he said Mm-hmm when he was inside Gina, as if answering a question she had asked; the set of his jaw as he grabbed Analuisa, as if her beauty angered him. Slowly, as I watched him fuck other women, I grew proud, a pride that told me I had become possessive.

I became wet.

Gina, I saw, liked to be blindfolded.

Then I could put it off no longer. *Charlotte*, he had called your file, *Charlotte*, the name no one used, and clicking, I almost believed this *Charlotte* would be someone else; I told myself I would watch for a second or two, only long enough to confirm it was like the others, and then shut the computer. But when I opened the file, I found it was not sex at all but dancing he had captured.

You in the little blue studio, working on some steps, a phrase. I lingered. This must be from your summer on the island, the last summer before your injury. Maybe this was even one of the last clips of you dancing. I leaned forward, chin on fist.

After your marriage, Luciano had started working on a showcase for your talent; something big, he had promised. It was never performed: You got injured first. But he must have given you some moves to work on, for now you kept scuttling across the studio, glancing at the mirror, scurrying and undulating, experimenting. Though the motions were ugly, they couldn't hide the regal swoop of your neck, the carriage of your head; they couldn't disguise the grandeur of your body.

Muffled sound. Johnny enters the frame. He talks and you listen, nodding, hands on hips, still panting.

Again, he says, and down to the ground you go, scuttling like a crab, doing what one man ordered for the pleasure of another.

More conferring, nods. Again. Johnny makes a motion with his hands. Again.

Each time it gets worse. The more Johnny talks, the more stiff and brittle you become. And yet even brittle, the song of your body transfixed me. The clarity of your shape. Watching you talk with Johnny was even more delicious. A decade or more I'd wanted to break into your relationship, to know its texture, and now here it was, with bad sound and shaky video but undeniable: how the two of you were when you were alone. The way you nodded, eyes on the floor; how Johnny tapped his lips.

Finally you wave him off, saying, I'm tired, and he gets out his phone and scrolls. Soon, new music: a nervy pulse.

My stomach clenched. Before my mind, my body remembered. Cool, hot: the song he played the day he seduced me. The same song.

He starts swirling his hips and swinging into those doggy arabesques. Then he's wagging his shoulders, encouraging. You do a few riffs, but you're still tense. He takes you by the shoulder and spins you around so your back is against his chest, and then he fits his ear against yours. As he nestles your neck, his chin on your shoulder, the dark warm wing of his voice pours into you.

Beautiful, he says, drawing out the long vowels. Beauutiful, Boopsie.

Then you're kissing him, as I did. Then he's cradling your head. Abruptly he pushes it down. Palm to crown, hard. Your neck buckles, a sideways jerk. He reaches for his fly.

I hit *pause*. The room rushed in, blue. How obscene, this pale sunlight. My pulse in my temple. My hands, strange.

~

THE SUN, so bright at midday, has been softening for hours, but it's a summer sun, too, it lingers, as if night will never come, as if I will be here in this late afternoon light forever. But of course I won't. The sun will set, Johnny will come home. I will turn a bland face to him and hide what I've seen; I will make small talk, and in the morning, with my duffel packed, I'll leave.

Until then, I'm writing you a letter, full of questions and pleading. Telling you what I've seen. Asking: Did you know about the camera? Is this how it began? Did you feel it ever after, the force of Johnny's hands, or was it the force of his voice, telling you how to dance, that ruined you?

None of it matters, Charley. Nobody cares. Please. Don't take those vows. Come home. Come back to me.

PART TWO

27

HE'S TIRED. THE TRIP IS ALWAYS MORE EXHAUSTING than he allows himself to remember, and coming so soon after Rome, it has made his body unsteady, replaced his middle with jelly. Driving back, he kept tightening his stomach, urging his organs to cohere, reminding himself that the trip was a success. The board agreed to reinstate him, and after all their texting, it was good to see Laurel in rehearsal. Important. Their drink afterward was nice too.

With a practiced swing he turns into Sykes's gravel walk and sets the truck in park. But after cutting the engine, he doesn't get out right away. Idly he remembers how Laurel flushed when he arrived, hairline to breast a pale pink. She's young, and much too starry-eyed, but there's something strong, fierce, beneath her shyness that interests him. That gaze she fixed on him when he said she should soften her arms. Resisting. Something crude in her dancing too. Not pretty, but arresting. He'll talk to a few directors, now that he's seen her live, get them to cast her. Yes. He flexes his hand, looking at his fingers. Hairy knuckles. No more exile on Cup. No more of this performative self-loathing, this public self-flagellation. No one cares anymore about Gina's post. He flexes his hand again, taps each finger against his thigh as if playing the piano, though he never learned. No patience.

As soon as he walks inside, he knows. Things have been disturbed. Yet it takes him a minute—dropping his bag, calling Frances's name, looking through the front hall to the kitchen, dark and neat (good, she didn't eat, though he's not surprised, dancers never eat)—to locate the disturbance.

His father's mackintosh. That's it. His father's old oilskin, usually buried under an avalanche of tech and performance wear, is on top of all the other coats, though it hasn't been worn in years. He smiles to himself, forgetting his exhaustion and jelly middle. It touches him, the way she is still so much a child, with a child's guileless transparency. Even if she wanted, she couldn't hide who she is.

Frances? he calls. Frances?

Upstairs, she startles, though she's been listening intently ever since she heard the tires on the gravel. There's a plaintive edge, even an urgency, in his voice. It reassures her. He doesn't know what she's done. He's eager to see her. Maybe he even missed her.

Boops?

Despite herself, her heart opens. It wobbles, made unsteady by the tenor of his voice. She straightens, and double-checks that no reply has come to her email. No, nothing. Her heart dancing, she descends.

Boopsie! Didn't you hear me come in?

Their eyes meet, brown to blue, quivering questions.

I was taking a nap. She stretches, yawns. I got so tired that I lay down for an hour. How was the city?

It was the city.

He swings from his back the flat Japanese bag he uses as a briefcase. He is, as usual, dressed in black, with big work boots and a wild beard. It's Johnny, she tells herself. Just old Johnny. She feels dreamy and strange, blurred, as if she has in fact been sleeping. When he looks away, she shakes herself. Wake up.

He is talking, lifting up a white plastic bag before her, heavy and dripping.

I brought something back from the docks. You didn't eat, did you?

~

IN THE PLASTIC BAG, slick white fish. Like everything else he makes, it's delicious, somehow milky, flaky, fresh. She eats with doom in her heart. That milky sweetness—does it not contain something cloying, off, tainted? Or is she only imagining it? The fillets, she knows, traveled for hours in that plastic bag, no ice packs, sitting in the June sun. With every bite she imagines herself cramped over the toilet, belly knitted by pain.

What do you think?

Amazing.

Little bones stick from the flesh. She pinches them with two fingers. All the girlish excitement over his return has vanished. The last video is looping in her mind, dizzy and swarming, Johnny is both sitting across from her and unbuttoning his fly, buttering a roll and slamming down her sister's head.

You think the fish is okay? She wiggles her shoulders. I mean, in the sun, all that time?

Oh, I'm sure it was fine. He gives a theatrical stretch, balled fists overhead. You know, I'm totally wiped. You don't mind doing cleanup, do you?

No, she does not mind, of course not. He kisses her decorously on the cheek; after he is gone, she shivers.

When the dishes are done, she goes upstairs. Sometime during her washing, the sun has set, and now inky blackness presses against the warped windows. He hasn't left on a single light for her, and she fumbles in the dark, gripping the banister.

At the landing she hesitates. No sound, though she knows that in the hallway beyond this hallway, behind a closed door, he is doing whatever he does when he is alone. She shivers again, and hurries to her room.

Since she left a few hours ago, the nursery has changed. No longer peaceful, no longer childish, it wraps her in a bolt of ocean, roiling and mottled and close. She checks her phone. No reply. Of course. It's the middle of the night there, and her letter, sent to the general info@abbaye address, must be sandwiched between requests for bulk orders of jam and questions about retreats. It's okay. She can wait.

In the vanity she studies herself. Surely what she saw today must be visible on her face. Some deformity or mark. But no, she looks the same. On the wall stretches the long neck of the goose, as disturbingly vulnerable as a young girl's arm.

From her pocket she digs out the keys. Warm, smelling of copper and sweat, they glint dully in her hand. She takes the smallest one, with its rainbow stain, and presses it to the space between her eyes. In the mirror she sees the face of her sister.

Tomorrow morning there will be a reply. Tomorrow, regardless, she'll pack her bag and walk the serpentine road to the ferry. Once off the island, she'll catch the train, go home to Philadelphia, tell her parents they must go to France, to the abbey. They'll demand an audience with Charley; they'll tell her the file has been destroyed, she can come home now.

Because—it comes to her now—that's what she'll do. Sneak back up to the office and erase the files. Why didn't she think of it earlier? So simple. Erase everything, then flee. The click of those icons into the computer trash; the pop-up box asking if she's sure she wants to empty the trash. Yes, easy. He might have copies, of course, in the cloud or whatever. But if she can tell her sister that as far as she knows, everything's been destroyed—? She slips from the ring the smallest key.

When she opens her bedroom door, there is silence and darkness. The only light comes from a high window spilling moonlight onto the grandfather clock. Its swinging pendulum frightens her; she falters. Oblivious and content, it sways like the swish of a cat's tail. In the silence she hears the whoosh of the blade, the grind of its machinery.

If she slips upstairs now, he'll hear. Tomorrow, then. Tomorrow when he's out she'll go back to the tower again. Retreating, she shuts the door tight, then carefully replaces the key on its ring.

~

SOMEHOW, SHE SLEEPS. When she wakes, at daybreak, she's sure it's for good, so fast and frantically does her brain start whirling, but somehow she slips under sleep's veil again, and when she resurfaces, it's fully morning, the walls dappled with scattered light, and Johnny is knocking at her door.

Frances, my dear. You're still in bed.

He stands in the doorway, a black column fuzzing into the blackness of the hall behind him. In his boots, he is massively tall. She sits up, rubbing her eyes and patting her hair, regretting that she's still in bed. Better to meet him with both feet on the floor.

He looks around the room as if seeing it for the first time. Touching the frame of the cot, he chuckles softly.

Then he slides his index finger along the mantel and holds it up to show her the dust.

It really is like a nursery. I put you in a nursery.

So you say.

He points. There's even a Mother Goose.

She nods. The goose's neck of muscle and feathers still disturbs her.

Without asking, he sits on the edge of the bed. Frances. Did you go into my office?

Your office? Her palms turn slick. Of course not.

He bites his lip, sorrow in his eyes. This innocent girl routine. I hate it.

I'm not, I—

Frances. He holds out his hand. The keys. Give them back to me.

Her eyes slide hopelessly over to the dresser. Seeing her gaze, he snarls and crosses the room in his big work boots.

Now. He gives them a shake. Do you want to tell me why you went through my things? I know you did. I can smell it.

When her gaze drops, outrage surges in him, strangely pleasurable.

Is this how you repay hospitality? By becoming a sneak?

Long and hard she looks at his flat face. She has seen it keen with ideas, and cool with indifference; she has seen it lazily amused with arousal. But she has never seen it like this: clinically focused, Dr. Frankenstein at his desk, while in another room the ugly monster of his rage wakes up. He is pacing now.

Johnny, she says hopelessly. Sit down. I don't like you looming over me.

She pats the bed, and with a sigh he perches again by her knees, his great weight spilling her toward him.

I don't understand. I took you to Rome! And this is what you do?

Three blue veins run along the back of Frances's hand. They are big and pulsing, and her anger, when it comes, is like the forking rivers these veins resemble, cold and fast and pumping.

I only did as you wanted.

As I—no, Frances. No. I explicitly—

Then why give me the key? Why not take it with you? You wanted me to find your nasty little collection, didn't you? You were hoping it would horrify me.

A moment ago he was white with rage, but now the corners of his eyes crinkle, he actually smirks as he says, And does it?

Yes. It's disgusting.

His smile turns icy.

You know, this is exactly the problem with your art.

My *art*?

He taps her once, on the breastbone.

This is exactly the problem with the way you dance. And fuck. And talk. You're too timid, Frances. You're afraid of sex. No, honestly, I've sensed it before. You're frightened of your own pleasure.

No, I'm frightened of how you go up there to jerk off. It's creepy.

He laughs. He can't help himself. The confused arousal on her face, the collision of little forces—there's something so sexy about it.

You know, Charley wasn't like this at all. She got it, she understood. She knew that sex is about giving yourself over to something bigger than yourself. She wanted that transformation. She wanted to be watched. But not Frances.

No, this is the thing about you. You're a prude. Everything you're doing in the studio right now reflects that.

She blinks, disoriented. I thought you liked my . . . ?

Oh, I do. But it's not—oh, come on now. Your dancing's lovely. But it's not like Charley's. She was something special. And frankly, I think this reaction to the videos explains why. You're timid, Frances, you're afraid of everything. There's something so *boring* about you, honestly. You're bland.

She takes a deep breath. Tell me. Did the women know they were being filmed?

What, you think I did this without their consent?

Over the bedclothes, she crosses her arms, looking again like a child: everything legible, right on the surface. He budges closer. Haven't you ever let a boyfriend take a sexy picture of you?

Only idiots do that.

He snorts. Jesus, you're so uptight. I had no idea. Come on, now. Didn't you find the videos a little bit sexy? Just a little? I bet you watched every one.

No. They're not sexy.

But as she says this, she remembers the slickness between her legs.

He slides closer.

They liked it. A woman likes to be watched. Like a dancer, she needs an audience.

Frances doesn't answer. She's somewhere far away. *Boring, bland. A prude.* Laughable. *You're afraid of everything.* That's not true. *This is exactly the problem with the way you dance. And fuck. And talk.* Each verb an explosion on the tongue.

Truthfully, she's not a courageous thinker, she always sees both sides. Her professors write on her essays, *Take a stand!* And for a while in ballet she had the horrible habit of botching her entrances, jerking and then freezing, unsure of the counts. Indecisive. Endlessly her teachers had admonished her to commit. Commit, Frances, even if you're wrong. But she never could. She was afraid. When the bike messenger had sent her away, she had accepted his decision quietly and cried her bitter tears alone.

Charley never would have done that; Charley would have screamed at the bike messenger, demanded he leave his girlfriend. She believed in her passions. She knew how to immerse herself. Up in the attic, practicing her jetés and ronds de jambe, no matter that the rest of the family was waiting to eat dinner. Leaving for New York at sixteen. Abandoning ballet three years later, giving herself utterly to Luciano, letting his way of moving consume her body. And then, Christianity. She immersed herself in that too. Not just a nun but an enclosed nun. Essentially a monk. And Johnny. She had immersed herself in Johnny. When they were together, she had given herself to him. But Frances has been holding herself back.

He's right about me, she thinks, in wonder and astonishment. He's completely right about me.

So you've really never let a boyfriend take a sexy picture of you?

Never.

He squints. Well, I'd like to take a photograph of you. Honestly, I'd like to take a video.

Ha.

I know, repellent.

Together they listen to the windows rattle in the wind. Reflected light dances off the water crazily.

He kisses her forehead. Wash up. I'll get breakfast going downstairs.

~

IN THE SHOWER she finds herself taking longer than usual, scrubbing her underarms and washing between her legs twice. She shaves and stands under the hot spray, massaging her scalp, before drying off. The towels in Sykes are stiff as sandpaper, and rubbing herself is like being licked by a rough tongue. She'd like to anoint herself with oils, but there are no scented lotions tucked into the bathroom vanity, though she does find some tampons underneath the sink. Which woman? she thinks wryly. Was Gina the last one here?

When she comes downstairs, Johnny is quartering an orange. Come here, he says, opening his arms, and she obeys, feeling in her belly a dusky dark excitement. For a while he simply holds her, running his nails lightly along her arm.

Then with his foot he drags the rug out from the sink and lowers her onto it. When he stretches out beside her, his hand on her chest, his body makes a warm curl around her.

She's always felt bland compared to other girls; to her sister, certainly. Quiet, watchful, cautious. Sensitive, she would have said, if anyone had asked how she saw herself, but no one ever did. Dance, though. Dance allowed her to say, Look at me. Look at my long legs, look at my bony arms, look at my swan neck. I am regal, I am delicate, I am strong. This is me. This is more me than when I am in my street clothes, talking.

As he strips off her clothes, as he gently parts her legs, as he gives a little gasp of pleasure, she thinks: How could I have not known this until now? He sees me. Their gazes meet. There's tenderness in his eyes, real affection. And something else too. Gratitude.

He starts moving inside her, first quietly, working, and then great circles of pleasure are rising up above their heads, elated halos.

In the aftermath he's shy, as he so often is, almost bashful. Could I, he whispers, nuzzling her head. I want a picture. Just for me. Just to have you, exactly as you are now.

Truthfully this is his favorite part. Right before their assent, when they are stuck, pinned, between their desire to please and their common sense. To see them struggle with their fear, and best it—that is what he likes.

She nods, not looking at him.

Carefully he positions the phone; while she was showering he checked the angles.

She crosses her arms over her breasts. Okay, she says. Okay.

Johnny draws a finger along her side. Beautiful. So sexy.

She smiles uneasily. And you'll erase it if I want?

Of course, Boopsie. Of course.

He begins drawing circles around her nipple with his fingertips. Uneasily she glances at the camera.

He sees her gaze flicker. Forget about it, he says. It's fine. Enjoy.

Gently he takes her whole breast in his mouth. He hasn't been this tender since the first time, and it makes her realize how much she's missed softness. Making love, that's what he'll do to her. She wants to give herself over to it, especially knowing how good she'll look doing so.

But at the same time there is the camera on the phone, there is the sense, impossible to ignore, that the cost of succumbing, the cost of this pleasure, is something that she can never get back, that she is becoming one in a line of women, consigning herself to a file, an icon, a bar as narrow as a grave.

This is stupid, he mutters. It's pointless. You're too uptight.

I'm not, I'm—

Oh, Boopsie. He picks up the phone, scans until he finds something, stabs and taps.

When that beat, that nervy pulsing beat, hot and cold, hits the air, tinny on the phone's speaker, desolation swamps her.

Come on, Boops. Let me look at you.

He pulls her to her feet and starts doing his little moves, wagging his shoulders, and she—even now wanting to protect his feelings—smiles. Encouraged, he dares more, lolling about. She watches him, wistful. Does he really not remember?

Here it comes. Spinning her to his chest, humming in her ear, he sings in the full rich throttle of his voice.

Beautiful. Beauutiful, Boopsie.

She can't help it. She giggles.

What?

You've got your little signature move, don't you?

Abruptly he pulls back and props himself against the counter. What do you mean?

Your big sexy move, huh? You use it with everyone.

His forehead creases with thought; in astonishment she realizes, He really doesn't remember. He's not cunning, evil; he just has a limited repertoire.

Johnny. How many Boopsies have there been?

Oh, come on now. Don't be a child.

A child, she realizes, is how he's always seen her.

It's just one girl after another for you, isn't it? Do you even notice a difference?

He's sullen now, pouting. She never noticed how slack and loose his skin is, the old man pouch of his belly hanging loosely, his dick limp and shrunken.

Neither of them stops the filming as she reaches for her dress and pulls it over her head, neither of them turns it off as she wriggles back into her underwear and jams her feet in her flip-flops.

At the door she turns. He is still standing with his back to the sink, gripping its edge as if afraid of falling off.

What, did you think you were going to make some kind of video art from that stuff?

He's silent.

Oh my God. Now the laughter really comes. Oh my God, Johnny, that's pathetic.

His head is bowed. She's still laughing as she pushes out the front door.

~

ONCE SHE CROSSES the property line and reaches the road, her laughter grows hysterical, and slides over into tears. Arms over her chest, she hunches, stabbing at her face with sweaty fingers. The salt stings her neck. She stumbles on a rock, and her toes twist painfully around the rubber thong. Stupid shoes.

She keeps walking, calmer now, though she can feel her sobs simmering in her chest, heaving and ready at the slightest provocation to come back out. Her sandals flick noisily against the gravel road.

Any minute now, she thinks. Any minute now he'll come driving up in his truck and drolly apologize. Or maybe he'll be kind, the concerned, paternalistic Johnny; he'll stop the car and wrap her in his arms and whisper into her hair that he's sorry, so sorry, he didn't mean to upset her, of course she's the only Boopsie, the only one who matters.

But he doesn't come. Once she hears rocks crunching under tires, but it's only a woman in an SUV. On and on she walks, down the spine of the island, feeling now a little foolish, kind of hot, her feet blistering, her bare shoulders beginning to burn. She should go back. Didn't she agree to the filming? Aren't his little moves, from a certain perspective, endearing? But that thought floods her eyes with tears, and she has to take several deep breaths, hands on knees. No. She can't go back. It's done.

Thus resolved, she turns more firmly to the road. Walking faster, her arms still crossed in front of her chest as if to keep something from falling out, she passes the tall grasses that grow over the old dump and the turnoff for Henrietta Beach, the floating buoys of the oyster farm and the pit where Johnny said the local ceramicist gets his clay. By the time Tess in her white pickup goes flying past, Frances has started to limp, her flip-flops sliding off her feet with every step.

Tess brakes twenty meters down the road and throws the car in reverse. In the bed, her two dogs pace, confused by the change in direction.

Need a lift? Tess is all smiles, but when she sees Frances's tearstained cheeks, her face falls. Oh God, she says. Get in.

Frances hesitates. One of the dogs comes over and tries to lick her face.

Yes, Abby, Tess murmurs. Who's that? To the girl she says, Come on. I'll take you wherever you want to go.

For a mile the women drive in silence. In the side-view mirror Frances watches the pair of big fluffy pups stick their noses into the air, their fur blown flat against their faces, tongues out.

Without asking, Tess makes the left in the center of town that will take them to the ferry docks. Not until she's parked does she speak.

I'm going to kill him.

Frances looks at her.

I'm going to fucking kill that man.

You seem so into him, she mumbles.

Tess reaches out, her old habit of touching, but this time she keeps her fingers a half inch from Frances's face. What did he do to you?

From across the sound Frances can see the ferry coming into view, looking hazy in the day's heat, as if seen through a telescope smeared with oil.

I shouldn't have stayed so long.

Tess bites her lip. I'm going to go with you on the ferry.

No, you really don't, Frances begins.

Tess looks over, amused. I know. But I will.

28

THE WOMAN AT THE CONNECTICUT STATION STILL stands with the erect, willowy posture of a dancer, though that is not why the other train passengers eyeball her and give her a wide berth. It's the long white dress that fascinates them, belted loosely at the waist; it's the crucifix around her neck, and most of all the wimple that attracts their attention. Men lower their eyes when she passes; children grow quiet in their play. They must think she can peer underneath their T-shirts, right to their hearts. Like that of a cop or a priest, her uniform has power. People, especially Americans, assume that she knows everything about their worst misdeeds, or else that she is hopelessly sheltered and naive, knows nothing about sex or the world. Why else did those teenage boys stop their talking and scuff their shoes when she passed?

The truth is that Sister Anne does feel a little raw out here in the world after six years (though she tries not to think of the world beyond the convent as the world itself; she insists, if only to herself, that the convent, too, is the world). It is so loud. Everything—trucks, trains, shouts, horns—is abrasive.

The plane when it began its takeoff deafened her, and she looked around in alarm at the other passengers, placidly nonchalant.

Every step of her journey has been like that, loud and chaotic, a blur of images made even more strange by the relative indifference of everyone around her. Talking has felt odd, her voice hoarse, English suspiciously easy after all the years of French. The abbess gave her the convent's credit card for incidental expenses, and the first time she used it, to buy a turkey sandwich (You have to tap, ma'am, said the bored teenager—he alone unimpressed by her habit), she had held her breath. Magic. Dark magic, maybe, but she couldn't be sure, things were so slippery out here in the world. (The secular world, she corrects herself. Not the world itself.)

Yet despite all this, and despite the basic regret of breaking the seal of her enclosure, Sister Anne has never doubted her decision, not once, in the twenty-four hours since she left. When she received that handwritten letter from Frances, that elliptical letter with its coy allusions, she had sat down upon her cot and bit her first two fingers, knowing right away what she had to do.

Or no, that's too dramatic, and Mother Mariama says that self-importance is one of her sins, she must constantly be on guard against it. So no, she didn't know for sure, it wasn't exactly that her sister's letter was an unequivocal sign. But as the weeks passed, and she received no response to her reply, a queasiness overcame her. She couldn't eat, she asked to be excused from kitchen duty, the steam from the sanitizer made her retch. Her back and arms ached with woozy urgency, like the onset of flu. Her sister was in that house. Bad things happened in that house. She weighed these facts against her enclosure. The work of her commitment. Then one day she broke down crying in Mother Mariama's office. Please, she had said, in her poor French. Please, I'll come back, but there is something I have to do.

~

ON THE FERRY DECK, Abby trots around, sniffing ankles, her big white tail held high like a shaggy banner. Passengers hold out their hands, and, regally obliging, she accepts their cooing pats, but Zoe, younger and smaller, is petrified from the moment the foghorn sounds, and stands trembling before Tess, who idly scratches her head.

Frances thought that they might spend the trip in silence, but almost as soon as they push off, Tess begins to speak. At first Frances can't listen; she's distracted by the diminishing dock, how rapidly the flagpole and narrow ferry office grow small, how soon the rocks blur to a line. All this time, she had only to walk on board. All this time, the exit was here. She's left behind her clothes and phone, even her wallet and passport, but somehow none of this bothers her. She's too happy to be leaving.

Johnny and I have been friends for a long time, Tess is saying. Well, six years, is that long? It feels long. I've seen him date so many women. After your sister, he went right through them.

Really? Frances says, listening now. Went through them?

Her mother used to say that Frances went through ballet tights like water. Her toenails grew fast and tore the feet; her growth spurt came early and stretched out the legs. Frances knew her mom meant the phrase regretfully—going through tights meant buying more tights—and yet she had felt a little prick of pride at her mom's judgment, as if she were wearing out the tights because she danced so hard and well. Remembering this, Frances wonders whether, when Tess said this to Johnny—*you go through women so fast*—it had pleased him, too, if he thought he used them hard and well.

Buried beneath this thought is a second one that she can't yet bring herself to consider: that to Johnny she will become another name on his list. A woman he has "gone through." From the chosen one she has fallen, joining her sister—her sisters—in the dusty graveyard of old loves. Someone he used to know; someone about whom he might say, I dated a girl once . . .

That it bothers her to consider this upsets her more. Isn't she glad she left? Isn't she entirely relieved to be free of him, and the island? Yet she dislikes it; she doesn't want him to one day tell his new love about her, to stand in his kitchen cooking for some new woman and talking about her as the unfortunate, distant past.

Tess is shaking her head. And every time, when things started to go wrong, he'd come talk to me about it. He had these theories. He'd say that one woman had a lot of trauma, that's why the sex between them had been so complicated. Or another one had been abused by a bad boyfriend, that's why she had trust issues. Or control issues. Or whatever. Sometimes he would say he didn't feel safe with a woman.

Safe? Frances laughs. Why wouldn't he feel safe?

He was afraid the women would talk to other people about him. That they would poison everyone against him. You know how small the downtown art world is. The fact that he didn't have any control over it frightened him. And I felt for him, I really did. I mean, it did sound like these particular women had issues. They weren't acting in reasonable ways, they were being unfair. I said that, and I believed that. But it got harder, as time went on, to keep acting sympathetic. And then with Gina . . . with Gina it was really complicated. I didn't care for her. She was humorless. Possessive. And she really did a lot of damage with that stupid post. Resigning from those boards, from the Hodge, it devastated him. And I really do love him. I was in love with him, and I guess I still do get a kind of excitement from being around him. He matters to me. He's been so generous with me. What I said to you that day in the church basement, that was completely true. He launched my career.

But, Frances says.

But. She looks at the younger woman. But Johnny—he makes me feel like a pill whenever I don't want to do something he wants me to do.

Frances, listening, wraps her arms around the shaking Zoe. Beneath her fur there is really not much dog, just a hollow body of ribs and hammering heart. Shh, shh, Frances says. The button eyes and goofy tongue of this small, comfort-seeking creature calm her. Slowly she flows back into herself. Oh, poor baby, she tells Zoe. You poor baby.

Zoe plops her butt down and puts a paw on Frances's thigh.

For the remainder of the ride they sit in silence, watching the wake of the ferry unzip the bay, leaving behind white trailing churn. Images from the videos come back to her, a swirl of skin and mouths. She tries to push them away, but they won't go, her mind is fishing through them, looking for something—right. The final frame from the *Charlotte* movie. Her sister touching her neck. Touching it as if it hurt. Mouth clenched, eyes shut.

When they come close to the shore, everyone stretches and picks up their bags, talking loudly, but Frances doesn't move.

You okay? Tess asks.

I hate him. I hate him too.

Then they are docking, and the passengers without cars gather at the deck's edge, waiting to be let out. Tess with the dogs stays back, so Frances is alone when she sees, standing beside the fence at the parking lot's edge, the tall white-clad figure who, squinting against the glare, meets Frances's gaze. Beaming, she throws up her hand.

29

BUT I DON'T UNDERSTAND, LEWIS IS SAYING. THIS is the thing I don't understand. They just let you come back?

Sister Anne smiles in the steady way that has discomfited her family all weekend. Not fake exactly, this smile, but so far from the Charley they knew that it makes them suspect a stranger has come home in her place.

It's not as if I'm imprisoned, she says. Nobody keeps me there. Everything is taken under advisement.

At the table's far end, Mira gently sets down her fork. More bread? Jill mouths, hoisting the basket, and quickly Mira shakes her head no. The last thing she wants right now is attention.

Already she regrets accepting Frances's invitation. Meeting Charley had seemed so desirable; when Frances said there was going to be a gathering Sunday afternoon before Charley left, Mira had said yes, she'd love to come, if Frances was absolutely sure she wouldn't be intruding—

I'm sure, Frances had said, toying with her hair. (Since returning from the island she has been so fidgety.) The more people the better. My mom wants it to be festive.

But it hasn't been. No one showed up other than Mira. And a weird fug hangs over the family. They're too careful with one another. They apologize elaborately for converging on the fridge at the same time, they ask Sister Anne bland questions and then nod enthusiastically at her response. Lewis's query is the most direct Mira has heard any of them be. Perhaps this is because Charley flies to Paris tonight. The time for being honest is running out.

Jill did conceive of this luncheon as a celebratory send-off for her eldest daughter; she's disappointed the neighbors and Gloria, Charley's old dance teacher, couldn't come. Of everyone at the table she is most inclined to be grateful that Charlotte—Anne, they must call her Anne—returned at all, and to see her connection to the church as something grand, mysterious, and subtle, beyond understanding, but undeniably worthy and grave.

Yet even she has to concede that everyone here, at the meal's end, looks less than happy. Frances's friend has been fiddling with her fork for the past quarter hour; Lewis, burly and prickly with subconscious awareness that feminine secrets are flying among his wife and two daughters, has become slyly insistent after his third glass of wine, bobbing his spoon at the women; and Frances, Frances looks most glum of all, hunched over her plate, where she's done little but cut her steak into squares and push them around.

Her mother is right. Frances is the most miserable; her hopes have been most thoroughly dashed. On the train back from Connecticut, and while Charley—Anne—sat in her room as Frances packed (We'll go home, Anne had said, I didn't even tell Mom and Dad I was coming, we should go back right away), Frances had avoided asking how long Anne would stay, allowing herself to hope it might be for good. And why not? Surely now she understood that what

Johnny had done, he did to everyone. There was no reason to be ashamed.

Then the gentle announcement that the return ticket had already been bought, and the awful, dwindling weekend through which they had all so grimly smiled, Frances running off to her room rather than show Sister Anne her tears. And the corresponding thought: So I didn't save her after all.

So you could have come back anytime? Lewis waves his fork at Anne. You could have come back for a visit? For Christmas, maybe? Or the summer?

Sister Anne smiles. I suppose so. But travel is usually reserved for extraordinary circumstances. Illness, medical attention. Funerals.

But none of us are sick, says Lewis, gesturing now at the whole table. None of us are dying. Right? Or am I missing something?

The three younger women instinctively study their plates.

When Frances looks up, Anne is staring at her. I cannot lie, she says. It's part of our vows. I told you that.

Frances shrugs quickly, impatiently, as if Sister Anne is being overly precious about a trifling detail.

Frances was on Cup Island, Anne says.

Jill leans forward and catches her breath.

I came back because I learned she was on the island.

On the island? Lewis makes scare quotes. I don't understand. What were you doing on Cup Island, Frances? You weren't with Johnny, were you?

Of course she was with Johnny, Jill snaps. She told you she was talking to him.

She never said that, Lewis mutters. She never actually said that.

Frances picks at her cuticle, but when she speaks, her voice is clear.

I wanted to understand what happened. I thought if I knew, I would understand why Char—why Sister Anne left.

Lewis pushes on his mouth with his forefinger. You were with Johnny? You went to stay with him on that island? What on earth were you doing?

And then, at everyone's averted eyes: Oh. Oh, okay then. I see.

He takes a savage bite of steak, chewing fiercely, like a horse. They all watch. Frances thinks: Something between us has just ended.

In the church one can be forgiven. Anne speaks sharply, more sharply than she's spoken all weekend. Then she softens. When I came to the church, I felt liberated from what was binding me. I felt liberated from the relationships in my life that were not pure or holy. I felt peace. Frances, someday you may find that kind of peace. But until then, all of us must remember. It is not for us to judge.

~

AFTER LUNCH FRANCES DRIVES Mira to the train station. A resigned silence settles over the two friends as they head toward the highway. Mira hasn't asked, and Frances hasn't said, what happened on the island, and they both know what this failure to be honest signals. Mira's visit is a culmination; after this, they won't ever be so close again.

She's nice, Mira says.

Frances scoffs. She's different.

She's so calm. I feel peaceful around her.

It's like she's been lobotomized.

There's a tricky merge during which Frances sucks in her breath. When they're settled in the middle lane, Mira says, You still haven't said anything about it, you know.

There's not really anything to say.

Something dead in Frances's voice makes Mira pause. There must be something, she finally says. Anything. Tell me what it was like.

Frances passes a red Volvo. I started dancing again.

You did?

She nods, and there's more energy in her voice than Mira has heard all weekend. Johnny got me dancing again. He built Charley a studio on his property, and I used it every day.

They pull into the station and Frances parks. He's a miserable person, of course. But he did get me dancing. She shrugs. Anyway. Thanks for coming down. Sorry, I know it was a little weird.

To meet Charley? Mira laughs. I wouldn't miss it. And then, at Frances's expression, she adds, Oh, babe. It's going to be okay.

~

EVERY TIME FRANCES THINKS of that ride to the airport (they'll all go; of course the whole family will go), her heart seizes up, as if by hardening it could prevent itself from breaking. When she returns from dropping Mira at the train station, her mother tells her Charley is in her room, packing. Sister Anne, she corrects herself, and a conspiracy passes between mother and daughter. Then Jill's gaze darkens, and Frances thinks, She's remembering lunch, and what I told them.

Restless, irritable, she mopes around downstairs, lying on one couch and then another, thinking grimly that her father, too, is avoiding her. She wishes she had her phone and then tells herself Johnny wouldn't have called, anyway.

Finally she climbs the steps to the attic. Their old barre is still there, bolted to the wall. A shabby coffee table and a pair of box fans are cluttering up the rug, but it's easy to move them.

Yet when she takes her position at the barre, shame floods her. She sees herself in Johnny's kitchen; she sees her sister in Johnny's studio, working on some dance move, and then on her knees. Obscene. Yet Frances too agreed to be filmed, to be captured like that, and now the gap between that self who agreed and the person who grew up here, doing barre in her childhood attic, is too large, she cannot bridge them.

Nonsense. Again Frances takes the barre, again she bends her knees in plié, but it's no use, Johnny is there, standing at the top of the stairs. Bracing himself between the banister and wall, he watches her hungrily. After some tentative port de bras (is he admiring her back?), she sinks to the floor.

In the corner beside the ancient stereo there is a stack of ballet CDs. Frances flips through them, annoyed at the insipid illustrations, cartoon nutcrackers and swans, a sleeping princess with yellow curls and rosebud lips. Nothing suggesting the power these roles require, nothing hinting at the discipline and striving needed to bring these ballets to life. Frances opens up the first jewel case, plugs in the CD player, and starts *Swan Lake*.

At first she's still thinking about Johnny and that downtown revival, with the men dressed as clumsy, wondrous swans and the rush of Johnny's ideas afterward. But when the Moderato begins, those eerie climbing minor chords, so suggestive of moonlight and lakesides, long mournful lines of women in white, she has to sit down on the floor and cover her head with her hands.

They spent so many hours here. It seems impossible that those hours could simply disappear. They were children,

Charley bossy, queenly, long limbed, and vibrating with plans, Frances a pudgy five-year-old fixated on tutus. And I adored her, Frances thinks. Though she can remember herself at that age only in glimpses, she's sure of it: For a long time, Charley was the whole world, and this half-refurbished attic, with eaves so low the adults had to stoop in the corners, and dusty air conditioners and broken lamps, this was our clubhouse, our secret world, where we wound ourselves in tulle and transformed into sylphs and swans and vengeful Wilis intent on dancing to death any man we found.

I thought I would find you up here.

Charley—Frances can't help it, she has to think of her sister that way—is standing where she hallucinated Johnny might appear, dressed for once not in her habit and wimple but in a loose black tunic.

Your hair! Frances gasps.

Charley touches her cropped locks. Oh yes, we're all as shorn as lambs. It's part of letting go of vanity. A wan smile. Which as you can imagine was quite difficult for me.

The first violin, high and plaintive and probing, spangles out from the tinny stereo, and they both think of Odette, a fictional swan-woman who, with her long curving arms and soaring arabesques, still haunts them. Even after turning away from ballet, and then from dance entirely, the girls are still enchanted by the swan who dies for love.

Or is there something ironic in Charley's smile? Maybe she finds Tchaikovsky's music cheesy now. Or too worldly, Frances worries, after all those hymns.

I haven't listened to this in such a long time, Charley says. It's more beautiful—she shakes her head in disbelief—than I remembered.

Charley comes all the way up the stairs and sits cross-legged on the floor. In such loose-flowing clothes, it's impossible to tell, but Frances thinks she sees under the robes fuller curves, larger thighs. So she's gained weight, she thinks, with a stab of loss and a prick of triumph, before hating herself for both.

They listen in silence before Charley says, Sometimes, when I first joined the convent, I would imagine that I was Odette.

Frances runs her hands along her knees.

Betrayed by love, all that. Betrayed by my prince. That's what I thought at first. And then after a while it occurred to me that what Odette does, in a way, is enter a convent. She surrounds herself with her sisters.

In some versions she drowns herself in the lake.

Charley wrinkles her nose. I prefer the version where she just sort of—retreats. Floating back into the wings with her swans, leaving him. She laughs. Pretty childish, right? But I was so hurt. Frances, I can't even tell you. For years I was hurt. And angry. Afraid to even look at my anger, lest it consume me.

You should be angry, Frances says eagerly. After what he did to you—

Charley holds up her hand. When we were traveling, we would go into these cathedrals. And Johnny, you know, would do a lap, pass judgment on half a dozen paintings, and then be ready for lunch. But I never wanted to leave. Sitting in those wooden pews, I began to see that what was wrong in my body and what was wrong in my marriage were related. They were coming from a place in myself that was not pure, that was not holy, that did not have love in it.

Basically, you didn't love Johnny anymore.

It's not as simple as that. I was bound up in this certain way of being. I had to relinquish it. I had to relinquish my desire for attention, all that need to feel special, chosen—it was all trying to fill a hole that only God could fill.

Worrying the hem of her T-shirt, Frances says, But don't you think you could do it here? I mean you could be a nun in the United States, you could work with the poor, or—

We are not called to a life of service. We're called to a life of contemplation.

Right, I mean . . . now that you've fixed this thing in yourself, can't you come back? Because I miss you, I really miss you.

It's not easy, Charley agrees. It's a difficult path. For me, but also for my family. I have prayed a long time over it.

Then there is nothing more to say. Frances closes her eyes, trying to imprint on her brain this picture of her sister in loose black clothing sitting on the red Oriental carpet beside the old ballet barre. On the stereo, the mincing prattle of the four cygnets chugs along, and Frances knows they're both thinking of those feet picking and threading the delicate steps with precision; they can both feel what it would be like to hit those counts, the snap of it, the pride and rightness.

You're mad at me, Frances says. You have to be mad.

Charley smiles, and it's not the sweetly soft smile they've been seeing all weekend, the one that has struck Frances as performative and has made her think unkindly that Charley is rather enjoying playing the role of nun, but rather a grin so incandescent with light and understanding and even—what is it?—laughter that Frances finally, for the first time, considers the possibility that her sister is happy in the convent.

I'm really not, she says. I'm glad you're okay. But I'm not mad. I let go of all that a long time ago.

The videos— Frances hesitates.

Charley shakes her head: No.

In my letter, the second letter, that you never got—

Charley interrupts. And I am so sorry about that. I told you, that account isn't monitored. I didn't even know we had it. But I'll ask if anyone knows the password.

It doesn't matter.

No, no. If you wrote it, I want to read it.

But Frances has grown accustomed to, even pleased by, the idea of her letter floating somewhere between servers, lost over the Atlantic. That's not how the internet works, of course, but that's how she sees it: as if her words have vaporized into mist over the sea.

No, it doesn't matter, Frances repeats. I want to just say this one thing. And it's weird, but I feel like I can only say it to you. Like you're the only person who might understand. The thing is, as awful as Johnny was, I don't—totally regret it.

An image comes to her: the wake of the ferry unzipping the bay. She is the water, smooth and placid before the boat plows through, and also the white frothing churn afterward, ripped apart but vigorous and alive, too, her depths forced to the surface.

I'm trying to make myself regret it totally. And I almost do. But not quite.

Charley tilts her head and shrugs as if conceding a difficult point. You grew up a little. That's important.

The phrase is so reductive, so small; Frances can't stand for her experience to be categorized as a developmental stage.

No. I feel like Johnny really saw me. He looked at me like no one's ever looked at me before.

God help her, Sister Anne blushes.

Not like that. I mean my dancing. He utterly destroyed me. But he made me, too. He gave me back to myself. That's what's complicated.

Frances, what you're feeling, it's normal. When a man is in love with you, he gives you an idealized picture of yourself, and it can seem like a gift. This reminder of who you can be. Who you want to be.

Frances opens her mouth to speak, and Charley again holds up her hand.

But the problem is that it's not a gift. It has a price. It comes with all these other things, his resentments, how he sees himself, everything. And that can poison the whole thing.

Frances doesn't realize this yet, but the words Johnny said to her, *boring* and *bland* and *afraid*, they'll live like a virus inside her, sometimes dormant and sometimes awake, replicating, colonizing whatever sense of self she's built. Like an infection, this kind of love affair can be chronic.

But it's also true that years from now, Frances will win a commission for emerging choreographers. On the eve of her debut, she will be lying in bed, turning over the details of the show, the tweak to the lighting made during dress rehearsal, the trouble the youngest dancer is still having with the counts, feeling both worried and deliriously happy that this is what she gets to worry about, before her mind will begin to wander more widely, over the Fitcher grant she refused, the alternate funding she found, the man she's been seeing, whether she likes him really, whether the joke he told at dinner was funny or offensive, how her dad is doing, did he sound muddled on the phone, is he growing confused, and that last letter from Charley, good, chatty, with an invitation to visit during Easter. Then, on the brink of sleep, all this will fall away, like the plywood walls of a stage house. She will become strange to herself. This is me, she'll think, and the thought will be disconnected from her work and the people she loves, severed from Johnny, who has haunted her for so long. She'll touch a deep chamber, a private well, a place she used to go as a child but lost as an adult, some secret self, whole and unbroken, an egg. This is mine, she'll think. Right here, this. This is me. It will be lonely, uncomfortable, this thought, and also liberatory. She will be free.

But right now Frances can't know that. She can't see the dances she'll make, or know that they'll be fully hers, not some gift from Johnny. Now she's just looking at her sister, yearning in her heart.

Stay, she says. Please stay.

You know I can't.

But I need you to say these kinds of things to me.

Sister Anne smiles sadly. You've always looked up to me.

Of course. You're my big sister.

Frances, honey. You have to stop filling yourself up with other people. You have to trust yourself more.

Oh, how Johnny would mock these words, how he would make fun of them, he'd call them—but Frances can't finish the thought because she's crying.

Sweetie. Charley reaches out and smooths away a big fat tear. It's the first time she's touched Frances since their hug at the ferry dock, and her hands are impossibly smooth and soft. Don't cry. You know I'm always with you. You know that.

On the stereo, the second act's finale is swelling, a triumphant bombast as the swans celebrate their queen's new love. There's bouncing swings, climbing horns, exultation. It's at such odds with their mood that the sisters laugh, and Frances wipes her eyes.

With a sly smile Charley swans up her arms, delicately, slowly, like the fluttering of two wings, until the backs of her wrists, at the apex of her head, touch. Her fingers still form the graceful soft net of ballet hands, and her arms have no bones at all. She turns her head to the left, and there it is, at once, perfect: Odette, Frances's sister, the swan.

Frances flutters back. She too knows how to make her arms boneless, her fingers soft baskets of air. Lips pursed to hold back giggles, the two sisters flap their wings at each other, first in mockery of Tchaikovsky's euphoria, and then more somberly, looking at each other as if looking into a mirror. Then the dancing changes again, and they are moving solely for the pleasure of breeze along their skin. When Jill comes to tell them it's time to go, that's how she finds them, two swan-sisters waving goodbye.

Acknowledgments

PJ MARK ADVOCATED HARD FOR THIS BOOK; I AM beyond fortunate to have him as my agent and friend. With Masie Cochran I had one of the best editing experiences of my life; she knew just how to help this book grow. The entire team at Tin House is incredible: Thank you to Anne Horowitz for a rigorous copy edit and Allison Dubinsky for a thorough proofread; to Beth Steidle for a stunning cover and elegant book interior; and to Becky Kraemer, Julia Talley, Laura Schmitt, Tiffani Ren, Nanci McCloskey, and everyone else who helped bring this book into the world.

The Oberlin Grant-in-Aid program funded a research trip to France, for which I am grateful.

Many choreographers animate this book: George Balanchine, Pina Bausch, Anne Teresa De Keersmaeker, and Ohad Naharin, among others. Some of the dances ascribed to Luciano, or seen at the Hodge, are loosely based on their work. Their art gives my life shimmer and depth.

A big thank-you to my early readers, Chris Leslie-Hynan, Rachel Lyon, and Anne-E. Wood, and my later readers Emma Borges-Scott, Will Frank, Michelle Huneven, Leslie Jamison, and Ted Thompson. Michelle, in her usual brilliant way, also came up with the title for this book. Thank you, Jessie Kindig, for the fairy tales. Thank you, Dennis Tang, for weathering both Ohio and a plague with me, for your cooking, love, and fierce intelligence. And thank you to my friends not yet mentioned—Ghassan Abou-Zeineddine, Natalia Boesch and David Bukszpan, Sam Cohen, Jess Gross, Evan James, David Mahfouda, Jessie Marglin, Amanda Martin, Katie and Thom Parry, Bureen Ruffin, Darcey Steinke, Bridget Talone, Wei Tchou, Anna Walters, Pallavi Wakharkar, and Han Yu. In talking to you, I find myself.

Boundless gratitude and deepest love to the Council of Siblings, Lauren, Mz, and Chris, who keep me honest; to Becca, Ash, Daria, and Ellen, who make our family better; and to my parents, Cate and Patrick, who believe in me even when I doubt. You are the best.

This book is dedicated to Assaf, who has made me happier than I ever thought possible.